D0105448

RED SKY
IN MORNING

RED SKY IN MORNING

A Novel

PAUL LYNCH

Little, Brown and Company

New York Boston London

The characters and events in this book are fictitious. Any similarity to real persons, living or dead, is coincidental and not intended by the author.

Copyright © 2013 by Paul Lynch

All rights reserved. In accordance with the U.S. Copyright Act of 1976, the scanning, uploading, and electronic sharing of any part of this book without the permission of the publisher constitute unlawful piracy and theft of the author's intellectual property. If you would like to use material from the book (other than for review purposes), prior written permission must be obtained by contacting the publisher at permissions@hbgusa.com. Thank you for your support of the author's rights.

Little, Brown and Company
Hachette Book Group
237 Park Avenue, New York, NY 10017
littlebrown.com

First North American Edition, November 2013
Originally published in Great Britain by Quercus, April 2013

Little, Brown and Company is a division of Hachette Book Group, Inc. The Little, Brown name and logo are trademarks of Hachette Book Group, Inc.

The publisher is not responsible for websites (or their content) that are not owned by the publisher.

The Hachette Speakers Bureau provides a wide range of authors for speaking events. To find out more, go to hachettespeakersbureau.com or call (866) 376-6591.

Library of Congress Cataloging-in-Publication Data
Lynch, Paul
  Red sky in morning : a novel / Paul Lynch.—First North American edition.
    pages cm
  ISBN 978-0-316-23025-4
  1. Murder—Fiction. 2. Tracking and trailing—Fiction. 3. Revenge—Fiction. 4. Ireland—Fiction. 5. Pennsylvania—Fiction. I. Title.
  PR6112.Y534R43 2013
  823'.92—dc23   2013021585

10 9 8 7 6 5 4 3 2 1

RRD-C

Printed in the United States of America

For my mother and father, Mary and Pat

The gods have taken alien shapes upon them,
  Wild peasants driving swine
In a strange country. Through the swarthy faces
  The starry faces shine.

—Æ

Part I

PART 1

NIGHT SKY WAS BLACK AND THEN THERE WAS BLOOD, morning crack of light on the edge of the earth. The crimson spill sent the bright stars to fade, hills stepping out of shadow and clouds finding flesh. First rain of day from a soundless sky and music it made of the land. The trees let slip the mantle of darkness, stretched themselves, fingers of leaves shivering in the breeze, red then goldening rays of light catching. The rain stopped and he heard the birds wake. They blinked and shook their heads and scattered song upon the sky. The land, old and tremulous, turned slowly towards the rising sun.

Coll Coyle was tight with rage and could not admit he was afraid. For hours he watched with dread the creeping birth of morning. Wobbled glass bending the Carnarvan dawn in rivulets of shifting purple, the slow retreat of numb shadow from the walls. He could not speak for a great bank of sorrow.

He lay awake most of the night, dreams snaking shallow and tormented so that for a moment he would find relief in waking, but soon the dread would pool about him in the darkness and a weight spreading heavy would pitch on top of him. He turned among the limb-sprawl of heated bodies, his daughter snug in his elbow and the press of his wife's chest. He reached a hand to her swollen belly and listened to the suck tide of her breathing. The surf at Clochan Strand.

He rose so as not to stir them, slithered and then scooped his daughter with feathered fingers and placed her by her mother's arms. The child awoke anyway, blinked at him with eyes confused and crusted, and he cooed her and rubbed his thumb on her cheek and the lids of her eyes weighted and shut. He looked to the darkness that held silent the shape of his mother sleeping. The hearth glowing red with sleepy eyes and he reached for his breeches and put them on and took his wyliecoat off the chair, sleeved it and buttoned it and set towards the door leaving his boots by the bed. The door sounding a gentle keening and he put it back on the latch and stood outside. The smell of Carnarvan like soaking earth. Salt faintly on the air and he sucked it in, looked towards the light that flaked silver on the dark waters of Trawbega Bay.

He stamped his feet and walked about the yard and opened the door to the stone outhouse, letting out the pig with a kick. Go on ye. The cow staring at him thickly. He yawned and rubbed his eyes and sat on the stone wall and ran his fingers over the rocks that sat jagged as if they had fought violently before being ripped out of the earth. The lime white of the house indigo in the light and he saw himself as a child among gragging geese and his father plastering dripping upon the blue clay.

Bones in the land. The bones of those before me. I will not so I will.

He looked at the house and remembered when they came—men from all over, from Carrow, from Evish, two men from Tanderagee who came all the way as a favor to his father. Towering, so they were, faces coppered and sun-cracked. The old man sparking his hands like shards of flint. Hardly ever smiled so he did though his body done all the laughing. They set to work, building with stones gleaming from the earth washed fresh. They stood the house, then cut sod and upturned it making flesh for the roof's bones. The men drank and cursed and sang songs till their slurring was feverish and they stumbled home to their townlands by dawn light and the family lay down on straw in front of the open fire too eager to sleep.

He sat and listened to the morning. The murmuring wind and the sound from the stone wall of a fierce droning fury. He stood and walked over to the sound of it and bent till he could see a hollow woven with web, dew-spittled and argent-shining, and his eyes alighted on a fly fighting the entangled clasp of a spider. The buzzing of its wings frantic and it became more furious still and its body twitched in trapped frenzy as the spider grappled from above until the life of the fly was spent but for its palps softly twitching and then it was still. Coyle bent closer and leaned into it and nudged gently the insect with the tip of his finger but the life was gone out of it.

He walked about the yard and saw the sky sheeted gray and stood thinking of the two riders that came. An idle saunter towards the top of the hill and then they had stopped near the end of the track. The loud call of John Faller. He walked towards them and took off his cap when he saw the other rider was Hamilton. Faller's smiling eyes. The height of him bearing down on that horse. His words plunging like a knife. Hamilton leering red-eyed. Like that was anything new.

Shoulda said something then. Shoulda looked him in the eye. Shoulda dragged him down off that horse. What are ye on about? What do you mean we are being evicted? You know we done you no harm. And the woman with child. Pure wrong so it is. Wouldna have listened anyway.

His fists tensed and something roiled in him like the white fever of river until his anger was foaming and he walked to the yard and pulled an axe grinning from the wood and started walking. He marched down the track from the house, shoulders huge and hunching. The earth dew-kissed and the coldness of it was numb to his feet and he wanted to hurl a mountain, to tear at the sky, to rip the earth open with his hands, and he turned sharp and strode to a spot where trees stood huddling. The axe swung in vicious arcs till a fir splintered and fell newly ragged upon the needled floor and he sat spent, his head wagging, and he had no power to hold back the tears.

HE WIPED HIS FACE with his sleeve and walked back up the hill to the house. The shape of his mother crossing the yard and the cow giving up her milk. He went inside and sat on a stool between the fire and the bed and looked at his wife Sarah. Eyes sloping off low cheekbones. A face built for sadness.

You were keeping me awake all night with your turning, she said.

Ye were sleeping.

I was awake. Where'd you get to just now?

I was out cuttin.

What was the use of that?

He rose towards the hearth. The fire alive in the rakings and he blew gently. Ash skittered the surface of fizzing embers and he raked it and kindled it with moss which popped and sizzled till flame lapped hungrily. He took flitches of turf and put them on top and watched the smoke sidle up the gable wall to lie sleepily about the low rafters and then he put his hand over the flame.

The child awoke and climbed out of the bed and went to him. He scooped her into his lap and tidied tangles of hair with his fingers. The child fidgeted and he put her down again and leaned forward on his elbows with his hands worrying his cheeks. Sarah watched him. His face a forest of dark stubble and the way shadows pooled his eyes like he was quailing from the light. He saw her and shook his head.

The door opened and his mother placed a pail beside the table and she fixed her shawl and went out again.

They ate brachán in wooden bowls to the spit of the fire, silence filling up the room. They each watched him in turn, his eyes upon the floor, and then he lifted his head and spoke quietly. I'm sick of yous looking at me like I'm supposed to do something. Fuck it then I will.

Sarah put down her bowl on the table. Coyle stood up. Is Jim's suit down at the house?

His mother looked at him. Naw. It's up here. Why do you want it?

I'm gonna go and speak a few words. Ask Hamilton to let us be.

Sarah looked up. No you are not, she said.

Alarm now in her voice, ceding control to his voice low and steady.

Aye I am. I'm gonna go and talk sense to that man.

Sarah got up and stood in front of him. You will not. You know he's not the kind for it. There's no sense in him. You'll only make things worse off.

He looked at her unblinking. Huppidy hah, he said.

She placed her hand on his arm and looked into his eyes. He stared at her, his hands balling white-knuckled, and then he turned and yanked open the door and stood there for air. They watched him, the child climbing crying upon her mother's lap, and they listened to his low cursing.

He came back in and stood with his hands on his hips staring at his wife and she refused to look at him. The old woman came from the other room with the suit on her arm and handed it to him and Sarah snapped up from the table with the child. Fool, she said.

His mother's mouth curled and her eyes narrowed like a cat. That young Hamilton, she said. A curse on the bodach's head.

HE SET OUT ON FOOT under sky sullen and uncertain. A back-sheared anvil rolled from the west and the faraway haze of rain upon the hills. He wore the suit tattered about the cuff and he wore his boots though he preferred to walk on bare feet and underneath his castor hat he was auditioning ideas of talk man to man that would settle things. Listen here now. Naw. I'm just saying.

He took Toland's pass where the world thickened in green and he came to a river spanning the length of him. He forded across a spine of stones and pushed up the hill in big strides through rushes parting and he found the track, walking with the power of a man of single determination, and when the sky opened up he did not stop, the track weak to the rain and his boots soiling in the softening beneath him.

The sky had more to give. The rain fell heavier and he stopped under a tree and hunched on his heels. His hat plastered to his head and rain dripping on his face. The suit was stained dark and cold to the skin. He listened to the tinkling canopy and a magpie's rolling rattle and he caught sight of the bird above, watched it flit the tree with its turquoise belt shining. Beside him the faceless yellow discs of hawksbeard were courted by a bumble-bee as fat as his thumb.

The rain softened to a drizzle and he rolled his sleeves and set off again. He met the whitewashed boundary wall of the Moss Road estate where the light was thin and scattered through the trees. Beyond he saw the sprawl of the country house. The land opened to vast-ness and he walked towards it, the grass a glistening green and garden beds of bloom. Stables lined before him alongside outhouses and the broad back of the house looking down superior upon the yard.

Coyle pulled his cap lower over his eyes and went towards the stables, silence save for the snorting of a horse, and then he saw his brother in a field with a geld-ing. The man's long face narrowed when he saw him. He clamped his jaw and looked over his shoulder and began towards Coyle with an angry whisper.

What the fuck are ye doing?

Coyle did not meet the man's whisper but spoke in-stead in his low steady tone. I'm sorting this out like I should have.

Coyle looked at his brother's shaking head, the ex-panse of jaw set before him like an obstacle. A flash in the man's eyes and the way his mouth tightened and Coyle saw in him his father's face.

Is that young bastard about? he said.

I saddled him up. He's out with the dog—hold on now you, he said.

Jim put his hands into the air as if that would stop him.

Hold on nowhere. I'll talk to the auld fella so.

You will not.

I've made up my mind. It's pure wrong.

You're right. Evicting yous is pure wrong. But if Faller sees ye lumping about—there's fuck all you can do.

I've been taking this lying down ever since that day I was too afraid to speak.

Faller and his boys will be over to yous later. Ye know how it is.

We'll see.

Go home.

Coyle smiled. Huppidy hah.

He left his brother standing mute in the field and climbed a fence that wobbled uncertain under his weight and he came upon the gravel of the driveway. Stones in their wetness gleaming and their crunch underfoot and then the front door rising before him in red. He pulled the bell and took off his cap and pulled a leaf of climbing ivy off the wall, rolled it until it stained his thumb. The door swung heavily. A domestic servant stood before him, her hair skulled tight and her blue eyes striking him with a look like she could read him pure.

Please, I need to speak with the master.

Nothing from her but the full length of a look.

Tell him it's Coll Coyle, son of Seamus Coyle.

Mounted heads of deer with marbled eyes watched behind the woman. He stared at her and thought he saw movement in her eyes but then she spoke, I canny help you, and she leaned her body upon the door and closed it. Coyle waited a moment and he rang the bell again but the door remained shut. He banged on a panel with his fist and he ripped a string of ivy. He turned and walked around the house, met the watchful eyes of a maid by the scullery door and he found his brother at the stables.

Where did that bastard go this morning?

I told ye to go home.

Tell me where he is.

The brother sighed then pointed. Gortagore. He usually circles back by Wee Joe's path.

Jim watched the broad shape of his brother's back as he left the field and he scratched his jaw and turned back to the horse.

HAMILTON AMBLED HIS HORSE on a hay track winding narrow while his dog bounded ahead. He looked towards the sky and the sun coffined in cloud and saw it tense with rain and he called to his dog but there was no sight nor sound of it. He followed the blackthorn-bundled path to the bend and beyond where he saw the hound and the shape of a man kneeling.

Coyle turned when he saw the man on the horse and he stood in the centre of the path. He took off his cap and raised his hand and when the horseman did not stop he walked alongside and took hold of the mare by the ring of the bridle and brought the horse to park.

Master, he said.

The rider heeled the mare to advance but Coyle held the animal firm. Hamilton looked down and glared. Blackshine of boot and corduroy breeches buttoned in gilt and the tails spun out behind him but his eyes were shot unsteady with red. Hamilton took hold of his composure and looked down at his boots and swatted at dirt with the back of his gloved hand. Coyle looked up at him, caught the reach of last night's drink from the man's breath.

Sir this isn't right what you're doing.

The hound giddied about the horse's front legs.

You listening sir?

Light rain began to encircle the men and Hamilton shifted in his saddle. His eyes sought out the sky and they sought out the dog and they sought out the track beyond where the man was standing. He leaned back and drove his heels into the horse but Coyle held it as it was, whispering to the animal soft words for confusion he saw quicken its eyes and then the animal was still.

Let go of my horse, Hamilton said. I'll not ask you again.

Not till you talk to me sir.

Hamilton looked at him and his hand sought in his

pocket for a watch and he looked at the time and put it back and then the gleam of a smile.

If you fancy your brother working for me again you'd best leave off.

Coyle swallowed and looked at the hound which had taken seat to watch and then the sky fully opened. Each of them stood as if they were indifferent to the rain and though that may have been, Hamilton finally snapped. He swung a leg over the horse and dismounted with force and with the reins in his hand he made to go past. Coyle swung away in the other direction taking a second hold of the bridle, the horse nervous and the two standing opposite.

I'm asking you to just listen to me, Coyle said. My father worked for your father all his life—died working so he did. We've done nothing but good for your family. My brother too.

Your father died of his own stupidity. And your brother? Well, he's finished here.

What's that?

I said he's finished. The lot of ye.

Coyle stared into the man's red eyes and the words came up hot and furious out of him. Damn your soul, he said, and he spat at the man's feet.

Hamilton looked at him wide-eyed and then a sneer on his lips.

Damn my soul? You've just damned yours. Your bones I'm going to break and your neck I'll have snapped on a rope. And I'll take your wife and cut the child out of her and fill her with my own seed and I'll take that other snotty scrag you call a child and bag it from a bridge and you can all go to hell.

Coyle's head clouded and his world interior closed to darkness and his hand bouldered. He fell to the man in front of him, his fist catching the other's jaw with the weight of his body behind it. The horse bucked on two legs and the man went staggering back till he fell upon the rocks of a wall. There was a pop softly as his head broke on the stone and the bone caved in, blood gorging out of him and his eyes rolling back as if trying to alight his vision on this breach flooding daylight into his world turned to darkness. There came a wheezing rattle from his throat and blood threaded out of his nose in little streams and it made confluent with a spume of spittle about his mouth. Coyle's legs went limp at the sight and he staggered drunkenly. The dog whining and he looked at the head holed before him like rotten fruit, the head lolling sideways onto the shoulder and he went to the man on his knees scratching the dirt with his hands outstretched and caught the other man's brain matter, viscous spilling from breached bone, and he tried to push it back in with his hands whimpering softly to himself oh Jesus.

SOFT RAIN FROM QUICKSILVER SKY and the land silent as stone. The water fell bathing gently all in its domain, the trees and the fields and the stone sill and the still seeping blood, rivulets running crimson towards the maw of the welcoming earth.

The land crooked and Coyle stood to his feet and steadied and he noticed the whinnying of the horse and saw that it had begun to leave. He looked around him to the fields and the path and went slowly towards it, the animal wild-eyed and he whispered to it, soothing then stroking its flesh, his hands sticky and staining with bloodied streaks the snow white of its fuzz until it stood calm and then he led it back down the path.

That's a girl. Good girl.

No place to secure the horse so he wrapped the reins about a stone and then he bent towards the fallen man. His eyes narrowed and then his gaze turned to the ground for fear of alighting upon the corpse's eyes, sightless bulbs glassy upon the sky, and he grabbed the booted ankles and pulled the body, its hatless head lolling from side to side, until the body lay cruciform upon the track. He stood catching his breath and looked out across the land, through haze the faded gray of quartzite hills and the bogland beneath spread golden-brown, centuries harbored and hushed within its grasp.

He squatted down and locked his arms under the pits of the corpse and heaved up the dead weight to his chest, the head slumping across to rest on his shoulder, and he kicked at its dragging heels. Ghoulish dancers they could have been, stiff-limbed to the melody of a whispering wind, and backwards he lost his balance. The horse skittered nervously and he tumbled to the floor still locked in embrace and the holed head leaning into him and he turned away and his stomach voided. Jesus. He got up and wiped his mouth with his sleeve and began again, squatting down and heaving till the dead man stood yanked to attention and then he bent again and put the body over his shoulder and carried it to the horse. He laid the corpse over the seat of the saddle and looked at the shining boots of the dead man then bent to the brush and tore at a clump of dock leaves and rubbed his hands on them. He turned and what he saw was the black dog watching.

Hamilton's hound stood at a distance alertly leaning forward, its tail standing and its eyes fixed narrow and unblinking. Coyle stamped his foot at it but the dog's gaze was fixed. He looked about his feet and leaned to the wall where he picked up a jag of stone. He threw it weakly, the stone caroming into the brush, and the dog held its ground. He picked up another shaped like a large fanged tooth that bounced dangerous before the animal and it fled.

Coyle went to the horse and took the reins and turned the animal and when he looked again over his shoulder the dog had returned. Go to hell. Coyle led the horse back through the gate from which Hamilton had come and closed it and eyed the dog watching from behind it.

The rain stopped and he steered a path towards the cover of trees and stood a minute and listened. Oh please be. The jolly whistle of a blackbird and everything else as it should be. He made a line towards the hills under shade of tree, this lumbering procession hushed with a slumping corpse coffined in nothing but the furtive air and it bathed for burial in ichor from its opened veins and no mourners but for this black dog visible. The trees parted and the land leaned down to Drumlish where they came to a brook, the water susurrous on the rocks like watching whisperers. He tied the horse and took off the jacket. The old tweed worn and fraying about the edges now stewed in darkened blood. He saw it and he cursed and he hit himself with his fist on the jaw. Stupid man ye. He bathed the jacket in the water and the stain weakened but remained and he wrung it and carried it in his hand and then he put it in the horse's girth. He bent again to the stream and scooped handfuls of water cool and mineral in his mouth and he led the horse and let it drink, the dog watching from the trees, the body of the dead man dangling on the horse's flanks.

They left the river and came upon a track and Coyle nosed out of the shade and as he did so the roll of wheels reached his ears and he caught the sight of some shape forming slowly about the left turn. His breath caught sharp and he turned and backed the horse into the trees. He watched from the foliage a man he knew to be Harkin, black-faced and bearded, the man leading a mule and cart towards a settlement of white houses that sat further down the road near Meenaleck. The parade approached with no element of rush about it, Coyle fearful for the man's eyes that stared dully ahead.

A snuffling from the horse and Coyle's hand reached around its muzzle to quieten the beast and his breath stalled and then the man was right in front of him, each step a moment that expanded in time like an eternity that was not his to live in. Jesus if there was a hole right here now I'd climb into it. His breath strangling in his throat and then the man passed.

THE EMERALD FOLIAGE BEGAN to thin and he left the shelter of the trees in Meentycat where the land turned to dun. Rough-stalks of flowered grass purpled faintly the heathered land and the rain fell cold and relentless upon that morass, black and receiving beneath. Upon the peated realm not a marker for a man and he walked till he met a broken tree white-boned and charred from lightning fire long burned.

He pulled the body from the saddle till it spilled under its own weight and it struck the ground with the snap of bone. The forlorn gaze of old hills as watchers to this event and on the wind the waft of sweat and blood. A carrion crow flew down solitary from the sky, black-dressed to sit upon the tree. It watched indifferent to the spectacle, took survey of the speechless landscape and cawed a single note of sermon before it cocked its head and took wing.

Coyle squatted and locked arms with the body and dragged it backwards towards the swamp and turned and rolled it forward with his hands. Dead eyes spun then sunk into the dark shroud of water. He gave it a nudge with his leg and watched the dome of the corpse's head shine faintly before it faded into the void of water. He stood till it was gone and saw a lone boot that beckoned from the beyond and he picked up a skeletal stick from under the tree and reached towards the pit and nudged it. The beacon stayed firm and he pushed at it again but still it stayed fast. The rain pushed down harder from the sky. He stayed by the pool on his knees, the ground sodden and his eyes sunken.

I canny pretend to myself nothing so I can't. I did it and so it is done.

The great weight of cloud rolled back to reveal a weakening of blue and then it darkened again and when he got up and turned for the horse there was no animal presence to be seen on that barren stretch of moor but for the unrelenting gaze of the hound.

How long the riderless horse stood in the yard unnoticed nobody could say. It ghosted into the stabled area, eyes wild and its bronze coat furred with thorns. The whites of its ankles were cloven with mud and its muzzle inked with blood. A call was made for Faller and the man strode from the house, his black boots shining and his cold eyes in their fixed position of smiling. Workmen huddled about the horse murmuring and some of them looked up anxiously at the man in the hope he could provide some assurance or explanation as to the nature of what lay before them, but he showed no emotion at the sight of the riderless horse. He took the beast's head in his long hands and looked at the crimson tapestry, examined the flesh of the animal for evidence of injury and when he found none he touched the damp substance with his finger and spoke under his breath in words that were as clear as day to the assembled that the blood did not belong to the horse.

Jim stood pitching hay in the shed when a worker stepped into the gloom.

Hamilton's horse came back and no rider on it and there's blood on er too, he said.

Jim put the fork in the hay and walked outside. He pushed through the men with tightening teeth. He put a hand to the flank of the beast and pulled the thorns from its side and spoke softly to the mare. And when he turned about the horse he saw the jacket rolled into the straps and he bent towards it and knew at once whose it was and he was struck with what seemed like a great and instant weight. There was talk of a search party and then Faller was at his shoulder. He issued orders without raising his voice then reached over Jim's head and took the jacket and unballed it. He held it to the air in front of him and then he walked to the house with the item in his hand. The men put down their tools and went towards the outhouses for their jackets and Jim took the horse into the stable. He guided it into the stall and rubbed its nose and took straw and lifted it to its mouth and he stood about and walked back and

forth and when he stepped outside there was movement
of men up by the house. He made for the other direction, went low by the back of the stables, found that his
feet were running, and he became weighed with the feeling that the natural order of things had slipped beyond
fixing.

THE MEN HAD FANNED OUT along the track favored by
Hamilton. To the front Faller walked slowly head bent
watching for signs. The turf was soft and giving underfoot. About a mile from the house the men came to
a fence and there they watched Faller bend to the wet
floor testing it with his fingers. He stood up and spoke
quietly to a man called Macken who turned around
with a face scuffed and shined like boot leather and
an empty eye socket sealed with a fold of flesh and he
beckoned in turn to another of the men. The three sat
on their haunches and Faller pointed to the floor and a
scurry of tracks. Then he stood and walked slowly in
another direction and his eyes alighted on the blood by
the wall and the spill of blood on the grass sluiced now
by the rain. He bent to the rocks and touched them with
a finger. Macken crouched down too. The other men
had stopped and stood watching. Faller pointed to drag
marks on the grass and then stood and looked at the
ground and followed till he got to the gate and stopped
by a clearing beside the trees and bent and touched the
earth with his hand and it came up tinctured with blood

and then he turned off in that direction and his two men went with him.

EVENING WAS FALLING as the men put foot upon the bog. The rain had stopped and a pillar of sun stood upon the heather as if asserting entitlement upon the plain. The two men followed Faller, who bent to the moss at intervals testing the ground for tracks seeing things the other two men could not, but they nodded to each other in recognition of the man's abilities, supernatural they said, and kept silent behind him.

Up ahead, they heard a dog barking and then the shape of a hound. Macken called out in recognition and not a word from Faller but his eyes were on the dark beast and he went towards it, the dog barking enthusiastically as if it were in its power to speak directly to the giant man.

Later, when the clouds had rolled over and the darkening pallor of evening began to fall, they dragged the body out of the morass. The horse strained in its harness and the sucking pool was reluctant to give up its secret, grasping at the corpse that emerged slowly in a dripping blackness with rope looped about a lone boot.

The dog barked and ran in circles about the men who stood by the ashen tree. The air thrumming with the electricity of unspoken glances, an awareness now that it must be a killing they were dealing with and not an accident and caps came off out of respect for Hamilton the fallen employer, every man but for Faller who kept his hat on his head and sat on his haunches away from the men with a pipe in his hand and a tin in the other. He pinched some tobacco and rolled it loose between finger and thumb then tamped it down and sucked the pipe patiently to life. And only when the cadaver lay stiffened on the ground did he go to it and put a hand to its face, wiping gently the sludge from its features, silt hanging about the eyelashes and teeth grimed and the mouth filled with black oozing mud and he rubbed a thumb over the dead man's lips.

A HUSH ABOUT THE HAMILTON HOUSE. There was the lighting of oil lamps and the sound of whispers that fell short on the breath with the approaching march of Faller as he strode through the hallway towards the east wing of the house. A gallery of deer heads watched impassively as the foreman entered the sitting room, shadows of antlers grasping dully at the ceiling.

Hamilton stood in front of the fire and he turned around and looked at Faller. He was white and naked but for his leather slippers and a gown that swung un-tied and in his arms he petted a stuffed fox. Faller reached to light an oil lamp and watched the man whispering into the animal's ear.

It was one of the Coyles, Faller said.

Hamilton stopped his whispering and looked up at the foreman.

What was that? he said. The old man's voice a stumbling whisper.

Your son sir.

Oh that. I see. Did you talk to Desmond about it?

It is Desmond that is dead.

The old man looked at him with rheumy fish eyes unblinking.

I see. Pity that.

He lifted the fox up to his face.

I don't think we'll miss him will we Foxy? We didn't like Desmond anymore did we?

Faller went to the sideboard and took a tumbler and poured himself a glass of scotch. A leather chair creaked as Hamilton sat down, gray belly flesh spilling loose over his groin, and Faller watched him patting the animal's head.

I have not involved the constabulary, Faller said. I don't intend to. And you have my word I'll bring that miscreant to you.

Hamilton put his ear down to the fox and Faller turned to leave but the old man raised his head again and Faller could see in the dull light the eyes of the man become animate.

Foxy says he wants his cup of hot milk.

SHE REACHED OUT TO HIM, put the child in his lap—baby skin warm and the bundled child with big saucer eyes and her looking up at him and enfolding his finger with a hand—the smallest most wondrous living thing he ever saw—and he sang softly in the child's ear a melody strange from his lips that he'd not sung before but it came to him easy as if he'd known it all his life and he stood in front of the fire with the child in his arm and he saw too the horse and rubbed its muzzle with the flat of his hand and she came over and rubbed it as well and she said words he couldn't make out and then there was blood from its ears, the softly plink of rain on the floor, and he told her to mind the blood but it began to course now, falling to the clay, and her face was wild, her eyes shrieking silent and he shouted to her and he put his hands to one of the horse's ears but the flow he could not stop, and she began shouting to him, and he could hear her now, where is the wean Coll, where did you leave the wean, and he did not know where he left the child and he stood there unknowing, dread rooting him to the spot and he felt the power of his legs leave him and the horse looking at him sorrowfully and he was stiff from the cold.

His waking breath smothered by mute darkness. The rush of forest must to his nostrils and he peeled his eyes to the starless night. His body was damp and needled and he lay in a hollow and then he sat himself up, stiff-limbed and shoulders planked and tense with cold. His boots were wet beside him and his feet were tucked under his knees and he rubbed his body for warmth cursing the loss of his jacket.

His cheekbone was tender and he remembered his

brother coming towards him outside the house that afternoon. The man in a rage. Sarah watching and Jim putting him to the ground with his fist.

They'll string you up, he said.

Divil they will. Nobody knows nothing so they don't.

Ye must be stupid. They seen yer coat. You have to leave.

I'll not be leaving.

You'll be dead before dawn if you don't. Go now and get away into hiding. Go up to Ranty's at least for the night. I'll make sure Sarah's looked after.

The night was still and he figured it long past midnight and in the silence he listened to the rumblings of his stomach. He felt for his boots and put them on and set off through the forest. He continued along a path away from Carnarvan, his arms folded about him and the ground dark beneath his feet and everything that was going to be enclosed in its own darkness.

He heard movement in the forest. The crackle of twigs and he stopped dead. A rustling nearby and he could not tell from where and his breath ceased. He bent slowly to his haunches and sat with his breath in his mouth. He listened to the wind whisper about the tips of the trees and heard the dull beating of his heart in his ears. He reached a hand to the ground, padded the forest floor semicircular for some piece of wood to wield but there was nothing to take hold of and the rustling came closer and he closed his eyes, squeezed them tight, and when he opened them again and listened there was nothing to the night. He waited and sat still. In his mind he saw his wife and his child and the child waiting to be and he thought of the trouble that would come upon them and he stood. He looked towards the crest of Banowen, neutered in black and the hills unnamed darkly beyond, and he turned back around towards home the way he came.

A GIBBOUS MOON WINKING AT HIM through the trees and the forest began to thin. The rain fell beaded and he curled himself against it and hoped it would give way but it displayed no such intention and soon he seized with coughing. He hit upon a path and followed it near-sightless and he guessed an hour passing till he came near the grasp of Carnarvan, the growing unfamiliarity of it, and he stood under larch trees he climbed as a child and stared at a field he thought he knew, a difference to it he held not in the spread of night on top of it but a way now of looking, and he came upon the lane familiar and followed. Dark upon the lane, dark under the beech tree, came to a bend and stood listening, the night that was still, scent of earth and sap, and onwards he went, upwards the hill, around the bend that elbowed the old falling wall, the sound eternal of stones turning in the stream, stones he handled as a child, and then he smelt it, the weight of it upon the air, and then he came upon it, and saw what was his family's house as it lay before him cindered.

———————

A WAY TO GO YET BEFORE the hours of dawn and Faller's man was sore on his feet. He was tired of getting wet and worn too of the evening's excitement and he waited long till after they were gone though he still looked about to make sure no one was watching and then he climbed up onto the cart. He lifted the tarpaulin and made sure it was dry and he laid the rifle lengthways beside him, shuffled some straw and lay down to sleep. In his dreams that came deep and manifold he did not register the figure of Coyle who approached the house in brazen form, nor did he hear Coyle kick through the charred remains of what had been his home for the remnants of bones of which there were none and when he reached satisfaction that this was so he turned to leave and saw then the child's ribbon, folded neat upon itself past the lie of the door, a ribbon once white now smoked gray, and he picked it up and held it like it was a living part of his daughter and he put it in his pocket and he was gone then into the night.

THERE CAME A POUNDING at the door and then the juddered sound of kicking and like a great suck of wind the door came off its hinges. The men darkened the house and the women were shrieking, the children burying their heads into the custody of their mothers, but

Jim said not a word. The men grabbed him and dragged him threshing out of the house. Outside he was stood in front of the dark figure of Faller, whose face flared to light when Macken stepped with spitting torch towards him, holding in the other hand a shearing hook, denticles shining like razored teeth. Faller took the torch and shone it in Jim's face.

Show me the cunt, he said.

Jim squirmed but the grasp about him tightened and he glowered at Faller who flashed a smile in return. He leaned in towards the man.

No? We have here a man who doesn't want to talk.

He put a hand to Jim's collar and dragged him to the side of the house and threw him face down to the ground and he came behind him and drove a knee into his back.

Rope.

From the house two men began to drag outside the women. Faller roared out to them. Put them back and shut the door.

He grabbed hold of Jim's arms till they were awkward behind him, forced each fighting hand open till the fingers were splayed. Fluidly he knotted with one hand the rope about each of the man's thumbs and then he wrenched his handiwork together. He stood up and yanked Jim to standing by his shirt. He walked him towards a tree and then he rubbed the dust off his shirt. Macken stood by his side and watched Faller throw the rope. It slithered and fell over the bough of a tree and

he made it taut and he handed it to Macken who sum-
moned another of his men. They took hold of the rope
and he told them to pull. Jim's arms swung up behind
him unnatural, a howl from his lips and the ligature
tearing till the ground no longer met his toes.

Faller stood in front of him, then leaned in and spoke.

Where is the cunt?

His voice low and familiar and they waited in silence
for the man to talk and when he didn't Macken stepped
past Faller and threw a fist at the hanging man's face.
Jim howled as his body contorted and Faller turned and
gave Macken a look that made the other men step away.
Faller stood still then reached into his jacket and produced his pipe. He looked at the man suspended before
him, his rictus face flickering in the light, and he took
the tin from his jacket and began to pinch tobacco. He
tamped it down into the pipe's chamber and put the bit
to his lip and he lit it and sucked on it slowly, the smoke
curling into the nothing light.

Now, he said. Let me tell you a story.

HE RAN HEART-JAGGED and bone-cold kicking wildly
through the fields, brush and briar pricking at his
clothes and deeper into his flesh and he did not notice
the rain hissing on the leaves. The cold gnawed toothless
but slowly wearing and he thought of warm things, a
fire to lean on, the pure gleam of hot food.

He was upon the place of his brother's house when he

heard the breathing of tethered horses and he advanced further till he heard low voices. Rough moonlight and he watched. Amidst the fanning of torches a gathering of men and the height of Faller among them and he crept closer till he saw a figure under the bough of a tree, two feet off the ground and suspended on a rope. The arms twisted backwards towards the shoulders, the joints wrenched seemingly from their sockets and the head hung low and then he saw the man was hanging by his thumbs. Two men were leaning into him talking and he saw in Faller's hand the shape of a shearing hook and only when one of the others stepped back did he see the face of the hanging man and realize it was his brother.

MINDSCREAM AND THE NIGHT pitched on top of him, his hurtling body a clamber of limbs trying to beat off the mauling darkness. From out of the abyss skeletal fingers of trees made snatches for his face as he ran from the horrors of what he had seen, briars like witches' claws tearing at his flesh and he fought them with blind fury. His breath jagged at his chest for each breath was a shard of glass and onwards he tore, through scrub and sheugh and down a sharp decline till something took hold of his boot and held it firm and the ground reached up for him and his mouth bit hard upon the earth. Pain like a searing flash of lightning white hot and thunder crashed in his ears and he rolled down the ground weak and useless until stunned he lay, his breathing fevered,

the earth wet against his face and he was arrested with
the image of his brother hanging from the tree like some
kind of Christ, broken and illumined among shadows
and he saw the image of Faller, the man stepping forward with shearing hook in hand, the implement rolling
easily between fingers and thumb, stepping forward towards the broken man, and nausea defeated him and he
shook deep with coughing. It held him for a time till
he could shake no more and he lay there sodden in the
moist arms of grief, the moon watching through gray
veil, and then he was upwards again, climbing into the
mouth of darkness.

RANTY'S HOUSE STOOD GOLDEN in the dawn, a lone
beacon on the pass near the top of the hill. Drumtahalla
this place is. No place at all and if it is a place tis not
fit for a goat. The Meeshivin forest spread wide below,
steeped still in night where Coyle had returned walking
stiff till he had reached the old man's door. He banged
on it with a fist and heard the scuffle of bare feet and
then the door opened a crack. An eyeball glaring and
then the door opened wide and Ranty stood before him,
small and square with a face cut from stone like he did
it blind to himself and he rubbed his eyes with sleep to
take in the sight of the man.

Get in will ye.

Ranty stabbed the rakings and forced upon them
some kindling and Coyle went kneeling towards the

reluctant flame with his hands. Ranty watched him shivering and told him to slough off the wet clothes and when he did so he threw him a blanket.

RANTY WATCHED HIM SLEEP. A stillness in the face that allowed him to see Coyle as a boy the way he was that time, the quiet intensity of him, grew into the same face as his father surely. The dark caves of their eyes hollowed by the tongue of the wind. And the pair of them when their minds were fixed as stubborn as the pounding rain. Dragging that body of Coyle's father out of the Glebe River. The wrinkled white of it and the life long gone out of him. Having to get that rope looped about the body. Glad the boy didn't have to see any of that. What he saw was bad enough.

He looked towards the window. Low light and the fall of rain like murmur. Rain that knows nothing but the pull of the earth. And the earth receiving it quietly.

COYLE AWOKE TO SEE RANTY on a chair by the wall watching him. The hard slabs of the man's cheeks.

Ranty nodded. Hungry?

His voice quiet and familiar.

Aye.

Coyle dressed in his damp clothes and followed Ranty outside. Rocks fisted out of peatlands that rolled downwards to the forest glistening in the catching dawn. Behind the house a steep slope and they walked up to where a heifer and a calf were grazing. Ranty went to the calf and wished her well the morning and tied a rope about her neck and tightened as if he were for strangling it. The animal stood legs outstretched and the veins on its neck thickened to the size of a finger and Ranty moved fast and with an expert hand produced a blade and he put it to the vein at the base of the animal's neck and made an incision. The beast gave its blood, the fluid draining into a piggin he held in the other hand, and when he had enough he handed the jar to Coyle. He took the open wound between finger and thumb and squeezed it together and then he took a pin from his belt and pushed it through all the while talking softly to the animal and made good the wound with thread.

He boiled the blood with oaten meal and they ate the blackened stew from cracked bowls and not a sound from the bare stone room but for the working of their jaws. They were finished when the old man began to talk.

The look in your eye I'd say you must have done some kind of wrong. I'm hoping you ain't gone and kilt nobody.

He looked at the face before him black-eyed with tiredness.

I only meant to hit him.

Ranty sighed. I know you well but I fear I'm better off for not knowing. I donny know where you're for but for a man running from the law I'd get myself to Derry where it's easier to be hiding.

I ain't running from the law.

Then why are you running?

Tis something else.

Ranty kept staring at him and Coyle turned his head. Faller and his men, he said. They got Jim bad too.

The old man straightened and put down his bowl and fixed his eyes unblinking on the younger man before him.

I know the kind of man that John Faller is and I know some of the things he's supposed to have done and if that be the case there be no running from him. So I'd be suggesting to you that you be done with this place for now and get to hiding in Derry and further abouts as far south as you can go or get yourself over to Glasgow for a bit for he's no man to be messing with. No man at all.

I watched and I did nothing, Coyle said.

When John Faller was a boy he was known one time to have twisted a whipcord round a horse's tongue, tore it clean out by the root.

Coyle looked at him straight. I only came up here for the night. Sarah's expecting. There's the other wean too. I'm going back so I am.

There'll be leaving whether you like it or not. If it's the family you want you can always send for them from someplace but there won't be much of you left to be having a wife if it's John Faller on the warpath you be meeting.

Coyle looked at him a long while. Alright, he said. I hear ye.

SOMETHING ABOUT RANTY'S PLACE that reminded him of the home he grew up in. Mote light dusting the dresser at the far wall. The place where he put the chair. He thought of that time the bird flew into the house. Panic mindless in its fluttering wings. Told Ranty about it.

I mind it was a sparrow though I couldna be sure. Me and Jim falling about the place laughing. The bird battering itself off everything in the room, bashed the crockery off the shelf and beat itself off the window and ma screaming at it and the old boy chasing after it, hold on now, we'll catch it so we will, gently now, and ma screaming just kill it will you and get it out. He caught it with his hands so he did, his face blank and concentrating, his breathing steady, one step at a time and the bird surrendering to him as he cupped it, head and beak poking out of his blanketing hands. Took it out of the house and set it free.

THE SUN ARCED DIMLY ACROSS the woolen sky. The raw umber stretched endless before him, the hobbled backs of the mountains silver-scaled and that high moraine thickening into angry heads of black. He marched past sightless rocks furred green and mottled by the rain, Ranty's blanket over his shoulders and his boots damp and the blasted land sodden and holed and bunched with flowering heather useless to nobody. Donny even know now where I'm going. Somewhere past Drumtahalla. This place doesn't even have a name.

The wind blew dry the clothes on his back and his lungs filled with coughing, the air forced out like a bellows and it stopped him each time and left him sore and shaken on his feet. A low cloud rolled lazy from the west where he could see Dunaff, the seaboard a silver thread, and a drizzle came down and he took no shelter for trees were few and far on this damned part of the land. He stopped by a stream and bent to the brown water and he visited a spot where a sheep lay down to die, its fallen bones undisturbed and its skull grinning upwards, and he sat a while in meeting with this ashen eyeless vessel, a monument timeless to its once-housed fleeting life.

Walking became the way of him and he ignored his hunger and watched the earth turn its back from the sun. Pure darkness some two hours away and he thought of nothing now but to eat. The hills rolled down and in the violet light he caught sight of a farmhouse, a faint dull white on the flank of a hill. He walked in that way till he came near and then he bent down low and pulled a reed to chew. He watched and saw no movement at all but heard the sound of children from the back of the house and he waited. Dusk stewed deeper and he stole up by the cottage and slipped open the latch on the outhouse door. The clotted smell of must and web and a high ridge of turf and the breathing

of a horse. He felt about and found some oats. Straw
bales piled to the height of his waist and he climbed
upon them and lay down and covered his body. Sleep
fell quick, dark and dreamless, and he awoke at intervals to the sound of steps outside and then he would
drift again. He awoke and found that he was coughing
and he buried his arm in his mouth. The door opened
slowly before him. A child.

The low light fell where he lay and he could not
stop the coughing and she saw where he was and stood
before him, her face all snot and filth and a fearless cu-
riosity in her eyes. She turned and ran and he cursed his
luck and made to move but the figure came back by the
door with another. The first child walked over and he
lifted his head and pulled a face and wrinkled his ears
and the child giggled and he put his finger to his lips and
shushed her and he smiled and she smiled back and put
her finger to her lips too. The other child turned and was
gone and he knew he had to leave now and before he
had time to stir he heard footfall outside, and then the
silhouette full-sized of a man at the door. The man saw
the stranger and he let out a call that came half muted of
fear and surprise, and when Coyle jumped up the man
reached for a pitchfork by the door. The shape in front
of the man sprang and took him to the floor, a threshing of limbs and then Coyle was upright with the fork
in his hand. He went to the horse and felt about for a
saddle and came upon the shape of one and pulled it.
There was a clatter as it fell to the floor and there was a

soft groan from the man and Coyle left the saddle where it was and took the animal which he saw to be a pony and guided it around the fallen man and out of the shed. Then he stopped and turned back and stooped to the man and took his hat which lay on the floor and put it on his head.

I'll pay ye back.

He stood in the yard and mounted the pony at a running jump. The animal more skeleton than flesh, bones gnawing into him and he drove his knees in tight. The child watched the stranger but she wasn't smiling now and he felt the boring of her wide eyes into his back as he dug his heels into the horse and evanesced into the evening darkness.

HE TRAVELED PONY-BACK throughout the night, his arms fastened around the dull heat of the beast, his mind slipping into slumber. No names had he for these places he was traveling for no track was he following, the man making but his own way through stretches barren where no man bothered to tread, the Donegal bog lying in swathes of indifference as far in the darkening as his eye could see. The moon fought the clouds and it was slow work in that haloed light, the animal unsteady on the hole-ridden moss and it showing no intention of doing what it was bidden. Bewitched it may have been as it veered rightwards instead of straight, or an intimation perhaps it was its own master intent on marking out some vast circle for cosmic purposes unknown.

The moon slipped behind a wall of cloud. Around him the land concealed in swathes of endless black as if the world had been turned inside out and his eyes strained upon the mute void but there was nothing to fasten the eye, the hills cloaked invisible, the stars all fallen from the sky in this no-light of the devil. He proceeded in hope and determination and when it began to rain he hugged the beast tighter and prayed they were traveling in the right direction. The pony slowed and then stopped and he heeled it in its lungs and it started off again, stepping reluctantly, and then it stopped again and he fought at it some more with his feet. The world silent but for the breathing of the horse and the soughing of the wind and he cursed the damn darkness.

And then the moon unfastened from the clouds and in the almost light he was able to measure from the line of the hills where they were and how far off course they'd strayed. The pony kept leaning rightwards and he'd fix it for straight but his mind began to drift and sleep would take him and then he would jolt awake to find the horse had resumed its strange rightwards path.

He cursed the beast half mad so it was and tiredness began to weigh heavier upon him so that he drifted into sleep for longer each while. Fragments of faces puzzled together and whispered talking in tongues never heard but in the mind of the man and he managed to stay on the beast, arms clinging tight, but then he was off a wall and he awoke with a start. He found himself upon the soaking heather and the pony a few steps away. He got up and went to the animal but it cantered off and he chased the stupid beast and nearly caught up with it but for a bog hole that caught his foot and when he was free he gave the pony chase but it displayed plans of its own that did not include this supposed new owner. The animal melted into the darkness and he widened his eyes but there was nothing to see. He was filled up with fury and he cursed again the beast and he listened for movement but heard nothing at all but for the flutter of a moth that winged near his face, the wind all skirling, and he turned and set off on foot, fighting the urge to sleep. He took off his boots and held them in his hands and took to running for heat.

To the east a flame on the horizon and upon the morning air birdsong scattered. The land leaned downwards and he followed till he came to a turf cutter's path. Sometime later the shape of a village hove into view and a thick spread of trees.

RANTY SAT HIGH UPON THE SHELF of rock in the dawn light reading the terrain like some exotic bird wizened and unfeathered. He lit a pipe and sucked on it and rubbed his eyes. From the edge of the Meeshivin forest they came. Six dark shapes emerging from the trees and then the shapes merging into three as the men he figured upon mounted their horses. He watched them come in single file up the crest of the hill and he saw the procession stop awhile as the leader dismounted and bent to the ground. The wind sang softly through the pass and he saw the smoke from his pipe circle below and with his heel he put the tobacco out.

The figure below got back on its horse and rode on. Ranty put his pipe in his pocket and watched the parade travel towards him. The wind bent the tips of the brown grass and the figures became silent men. They were dressed for the rain with oilskins on their backs and each one by his side had the long snout of a musket. Two of their faces he did not know but the front man he recognized by the size of his frame and the stovepipe hat he wore and he studied the way the man sat different than the others sharing grace with his beast. Ranty perched quiet and watched the men come to a stop near the mouth of the Drumtahalla pass and take a turn right and upwards on a small track that led narrow to a house he knew to be his own.

His eyes followed the backs of the men and alighted on the leader who brought his horse to a stop and who then called out without making a turn in a voice that rung out clear.

You'll be coming down from there old man.

I WAS BORN IN ROUGH WEATHER so I was and that's what you come to expect. There's no sky so blue that it won't turn dark and no cloud I've seen yet that donny carry rain. That's just the way of it. The last time I seen Coll were that day, and it was later that night when Faller and his men come looking for him. A day that began like most others. I remember seeing that the bay was dead calm like it hadn't a bother on it and I was wondering about what kind of summer we were to have, if it was to be a repeat of the summer before when the cows were going dunty in the fields what with the heat and all them flies. Dunty so they were.

It had been after raining so it was and I saw out the window Coll's brother Jim coming up the hill, something in his face, and I thought he was coming to tell me something bad and I went out to meet him and next thing I saw Coll was there too. I'd never seen him at all, and Jim just began shoutin and he put his hands about Coll's neck roarin, the head on him like he was the divil himself all red and spittin. And I ain't never seen him like that and Coll not sayin a word just standin there with his hands by his side lookin at him dead-eyed, dead-eyed so he was.

They were like different men. All them years I was courtin Coll and the few years married to him and I never saw him like it. Jim pushed him to the ground and Coll got up and his temper snapped and they started fightin and the child was in my arms and she started to cry and I had to put her down, ran towards them so I did but I was hit to the ground by one of them, I donny know who, and when I got up it was over, Jim had begun walking off holding his hands to his head.

I'll never forget Coll's face that time. There was blood on him and he was clagged in dirt so he was and he stopped and looked at the wee one who was standin cryin by the door and he turned to me and that look—ach I felt it like it was razors put to my own heart. I seen that look in him once before. That was before I took with him and when he was only a boy—twas the time his father was kilt and they hauled his body out of the Glebe River. He'd been trying to rescue a horse that young Hamilton scared into the water. They said the boy scared the horses after firing a gun he'd been playing with. Coll ran off when he saw what happened—watched the whole thing unfold so he did—and they said he never came home that night from the shock of it, spent the night in the forest on his own, and then he came home the next morning just a wee lad by himself.

They said Faller would let that Hamilton boy get away with murder, always up to badness so he was. And there were some said Faller was more like a father to him than his own, that his mother when she were alive spent more time with Faller than she should have, but I donny know nothin about that. Faller used to go away for months at a time and nobody knew where he went.

And when he'd come back, that Hamilton boy would be trailing after him like a dog.

All I know is that business at the river was never over in Coll's head. Sure he always went out of his way to avoid workin for Hamilton even if it meant going away for the summer. And he used to row with Jim about it all the time, the way Jim had no bother with workin on the estate. But still, Coll never did nothin to rouse Hamilton. It wasn't the kind of him. Wasn't the kind of him at all. And that's what was so confusing when Hamilton wanted us out. I never could figure the reason for it.

MAKE YOURSELF AT HOME old man. Sit down.

Faller took the chair by the table and Ranty did as he was told, reaching out for the other chair with slowness in his bones. His throat tight and his eyes fixed on the man before him upright in the seat.

Scant light in the room to see. Ranty narrowed his eyes and saw Macken in shadow by the door, caught sight of the man's single eye fixed on him and by the window in silhouette there stood the other whose body blocked what little there was of the light, the man unknown to him, arms folded beneath a low-slung castor hat.

Faller sat looking at Ranty with his tongue pressing into his lower lip. Then he rubbed at a moustache that hung long over his mouth and smiled.

Did you know old man the Irish never founded a

town? Never founded a town. I'll bet you didn't. But it's true. The Danes and the Normans came here and cut down your forests. They founded on those clearings every single Irish town that exists. Had to build them themselves. Dublin, Wexford, Wicklow, Limerick, Cork. You've got the Danes to thank for all of that. Perhaps you've never seen them yourself, stuck here like you are, an old rock on the top of this hill. But I can assure you old man the Danes did a fine job. Dublin especially. You've seen Dublin haven't you Macken? You will vouch that it is a fine town?

The man by the door grunted and then walked over to the fire and spat into it. Faller's eyes dancing now and his tongue pressed again into his lower lip and when he spoke his voice swayed with amusement.

The Danes and the Normans they built your roads too. The Irish never even founded a road. Imagine that. Thousands of years trudging in the rain and the mud, back and forth, to and fro, in your bare feet, up to your knees in cow shit. It must have been slow going that on your primitive paths. And nobody not once thought of making a road. You had to be helped with that too, didn't you?

Faller turned around to the young man by the window and instructed him to go out to the horse and fetch him the rope. The room brightened. Then he turned and looked at the old man.

Not that you knew much about building either. You lived in your bothies made of clay and branches. You lived like that for thousands of years. But you could hardly call that living now could you old man? You had to be shown how to secure a proper roof over your heads. What I'm saying about all this is that you needed guidance.

Faller stood up out of the chair and leaned to the fire. He took the poker and stabbed at the turf and he put his hands towards the flame and rubbed them slowly.

When you think about it old man, you do have to wonder what the Irish were doing all those years. Imagine. What a state you would be in if left to your own devices. You really do have to think about that. To think of the advancement of the amenities of life. Well. I'll tell you what you were doing old man. You were standing about in the rain up to your oxters in cow shit. The world pissing on your heads. Huddling in your dank forests. Squirming about in your little wooden huts. Stealing each other's cows then murdering each other for it. It's not what you would call civilization is it old man? No. I think not.

Gillen returned and closed the door and went to the window where his body smothered the available light. Faller stared into the rheumy eyes of Ranty, saw they were alighted now by something different than the worry he saw earlier on, saw it was dread, and he watched the old man chafing his hands under the table. He sat back down on the chair and his voice dropped to a whisper. He leaned into him, as if to benefit the man with a confidence.

It has to be said, none of this matters at all to me. But you do see the point. What I'm saying is you've always needed help. Needed guidance. And do you know what old man? That's what I'm here for. I'm here to help you. To guide you. To show you what's what.

Faller called to Gillen and took the rope from his hand and put it on the table. The room silent but for the working of the fire. Ranty turned his head from the eyes of Faller and forced a cough into his hand. Then he spoke in a quiet voice.

What's all that talk about? You're as much from this place as any man. Not a drop of foreign blood in ye.

Faller put his hands flat on the table and leaned into Ranty.

I'm not like you, he said.

He lifted a long finger and drummed it off his own forehead.

I don't think like you.

He stood up and turned to his men.

Give me a few moments alone with the old man. I am going to help show him what I mean by guidance.

HE CAME TO A RIVER gurgling over rocks that fell to rest in a pool. His body dull with hunger and he lay down on the bank, a bed of ferns waiting uncoiled to receive him bending under his weight. He lay on his side and watched the waters glassy on the bank, stared deep into the swirling rusted pool. His mind sagged for it was sleep he wanted more than anything else and he slipped into slumber, the soothing of distant voices and the ceasing of time to be.

When he awoke he sat himself upright for a while in thinking, began to accept that things were gone beyond fixing, and he leaned over the river and dipped his hands. A quick coldness and he doused his face with it and rubbed his eyes and stared into the pool. He rummaged and found a broken branch and peeled dead flesh and he found a stone and sharpened his stick into a pike. He leaned out over the bank and held his breath and pierced slowly the surface of the water, his eyes peeled to the liquid darkness. He waited and saw nothing and began to think of sleep and he stood and shook himself awake. He walked in quick circles on the bank and flapped his arms and doused his face again with water and then he kneeled down with the pike and waited.

He saw himself on the surface and pierced it gently with his pike and he saw his brother as a youngster beside him, the pair of them leaning and ducking their sticks and then Jim bringing an eel squirming to the surface and he thought of his brother now and winced. Why didn't I do something? Could have done something. Could have waited and cut him down at least.

He waited and watched, the water slowly swirling, and then he drove down his rod decisive. An eel bedded was broken and brought buckling to the bank, a squirming serpent silver-bellied. He dropped it down fine and fat, its fangs snapping at the air. The flesh was oiled and glistening and the creature shook itself out of its confusion and made towards the water as if some keener intelligence other than instinct was at work and he yanked it by the tail and swung it deeper into the bank. He reached down and closed his palm about the creature's neck and took a stone and hit it. The shape of the head holding firm but the body quickening into spasm and he sat on the grass and watched the life leave its body.

No knife for cutting and no way to eat it but to eat it raw. He sat on a stone with his back to the trees and sunk his teeth into the meat. Flesh stiff and unctuous in his mouth and he chewed it slowly. And then he heard the rustle of the man behind him, the man who had been watching him the whole time, and he turned with shock and made as if to run, the eel falling out of his lap, but he caught sight of the man just smiling and Coyle found himself standing.

The stranger was small, the top of his head reaching no further than Coyle's chest. His head was too small for his shoulders and his ears too small for his head that sat smooth as an egg. He had a crooked-toothed grin and a bag in his hand.

Are ye trying to scare me? asked Coyle.

I ain't seen a grown man catch an eel like that and I certainly ain't seen him trying to eat one the way you're going about it.

I left the fire at home so I did.

The stranger motioned his head and pointed behind him towards the forest.

Come with me if ye want to be cooking it. I've got a wee house.

Coyle stood and watched the stranger disappear into the trees.

He called out. Are we near Ballycallan?

A voice reached him laughing from the trees. Ballycallan? Yer way off. This here's Meenaderry.

I donny even know where I am anymore.

THE PATH WAS NO PATH. The stranger steered as if arbitrary, a zigzag of scurried feet to stop and meet with the mossy floor where he picked and bagged brown mushrooms. Coyle followed, the eel slumped in his hand, and they walked further into the forest, the reaching light growing fainter and the river dimly heard. Overhead birds flapped and settled and he listened to a pair furiously chatter and wondered what they were and he stopped and looked to the branches and when he looked around again the stranger had gone. He walked on ahead but there was no man to be seen and he peered into the gloom, the forest offering no path nor the shape of any man. He walked further and stopped and turned and he looked at the eel and took a bite out of it bitter and stood chewing. He began to walk back the way he came when he heard the voice call behind him.

Don't be getting lost now.

Coyle turned around and saw the stranger walk then

bend to gather mushrooms by a tree and then he was up again and pointing in the direction Coyle was to follow.

If you'd keep still a minute I might find ye.

The forest crackled around them and the sky scratched through. They steered around a great fallen fir claimed by moss and rot and then there came a small clearing and half strangled in green the shape of a house. He stood outside and coughed into his arm and the man opened the latch and stood in the doorway waiting for Coyle to finish.

This here's a stranger who's going to be eating with us.

Stale cat piss nauseous on the air and a young woman took shape from shadow. She stood bone-thin and no more than sixteen, a head too small for shoulders like the stranger beside him and her hair a mussing growth of fawn. Coyle stood scuff-faced and dirty and she stared at the guest and took the bag from the man and emptied its contents, the air dusted with spore. The stranger pointed to a chair and Coyle sat down and a young boy crawled over to him and stood up. No fear in this child's eyes. A strange one. And then the child rubbed his nose and turned to play with the kitten.

Gimme here that eel of yours.

Coyle looked at the stranger. Can't see into the man's eyes. What's he hiding? Reminds me of Mickey Joebilly the way he moves. Joebilly always sneaking about the place to rob ye. The man produced a knife and took the eel from him and he put it flat on the table. He drove a nail into its head and angled the knife blade into the neck and halved it open lengthways and he tossed the innards into the middle of the floor where it was leaped upon by cats.

He chopped the fish meat and wiped away the blood and oil with the back of his hand and Coyle went to the fire and hugged over it and he fought the urge to cough but it took hold of him again and when he was finished he found the pair were watching. The girl fed the fire and the eel was cooked in stew and Coyle grabbed a bowl and ate the watery food and when he was done he asked if he could sleep a while and the stranger assented even though the day was still young.

The sun slid slowly down the sky and when it was nightfall the stranger said not a word and let the guest stay as he was still asleep by the fire.

HE AWOKE IN THE LOST HOURS of night, the fire asleep and a hush upon the house. Need to get away from this place. Need to take a piss. He readied to get up when he heard moaning from the other side of the room. The soft scufflings of sex and the stranger's low grunt and he turned his body quietly away. Jesus. The man panting like some kind of animal and he lay there for some time trying to ignore the sounds in the room till he felt a tickle in his chest and he eased his breathing but the assault came anyway. He sat up and coughed deep till he was spent and fell back upon the straw and the sounds ceased, to be replaced by whispering and then the voices stopped and he lay awake wondering how long they'd be listening to each other.

THE STRANGER WAS GONE and just herself in the room and he sat up and said he'd be going. She told him to stay and said she had made him some food and she brought it to him in a bowl. Oats warm and soaking. She watched him eat and when he was finished she sat down beside him. A gulf of silence between them and then she leaned towards him. Cold?

He ignored the question. She began to rub his back and he tensed at her touch and she moved to his shoulders and put a mouth to his ear. Lie with me.

He looked at her with alarm and saw into her eyes, a softening of sea green, and she put a hand on his back again but he freed himself with a shake. He turned away awkward and she stood up and faced him and took a hold of the hem of her smock and hoicked it up to her shoulders. Breasts white as two pails of milk.

Take me, she said.

Put yer dress back on.

She walked forward. Ye can take me.

I donny want to take you.

Please, she said.

He turned away from her and she pleaded again and he shot to his feet and took hold of her and yanked the dress back down. She lashed her arms around his neck and tried to kiss his face but he shook her free and pushed her to the floor. He turned and saw the young child was watching. The boy looked at him with ugly eyes and ran to his mother and pulled at her clothes and when she got to her knees she slapped the boy across the face and the child went away wailing. She sat on a stool and stared at Coyle. A hurt expression marked her face and he shook his head and made for the door. She beat him to it and stood in front of it, apologetic now, asking for him to stay and when he said no she said it's raining now, you can't go out in that, and he looked at her with incomprehension. He told her, no, he had to go now and he asked her to move aside but she shook her head and he looked at the child and blushed and the child looked at him afraid and he put his hands to his hips and sat down. He watched the fire vacantly, warmed his hands and looked at the cats curled variously about the room and then he saw her sit down and he took his chance, grabbed his blanket and he was up at a run taking in his hand the latch of the door.

RAINFALL MADE MUST the scent of moss. A foot-worn path away from the house and he followed it and when he was out of sight he stopped by a rock and sat down. He put his head in his hands then wiped his nose with the back of his sleeve. The conversational pitter of dripping leaf and stale cat piss in his nostrils. That girl's crazy green eyes.

He sat awhile for figuring till he heard movement coming down the path. Through the trees he made out the head of the stranger and he heard him talking excitedly and he ducked instinctively to the ground with his blanket and clambered till he was hiding behind a tree, the moss moist to his knees. He heard the snuffle of horses and he lifted his head up to see three men on horseback behind the stranger. He snouted the ground, his heart clanging, and he held his breath as the men filed past and he fought the urge to run. When they had passed he moved with stealth and crept back towards the house. He watched the men dismount silently and each tie his horse to a tree and the stranger told the men to wait and he went up to the door and opened it. Faller stood with his hands on his hips as the stranger went inside and there came a roaring from the house and the sound of a woman wailing. The stranger came outside and he was waving his arms saying to the men I told her to keep em there just in case. I knew he might be somebody.

Faller eyed the stranger with no expression on his face.

Will you still pay me? the stranger asked.

You're not a man of your word, said Faller.

She said she'd keep em. I showed you where he was. He must be hereabouts.

Show me him then.

The stranger shrugged and Faller stepped forward and the man stepped back till he was up against the wall and he craned his neck towards the door and he called out. How long ago did he leave?

The men heard sobbing and the girl stepped out with the boy hanging by her knees and she said just a wee while.

Faller looked at the girl and he looked down at the stranger and he looked at the girl again and he saw the child and his eyes narrowed. Macken turned to him. Well he ain't gone down the path we just been on.

Faller turned and pointed. Gillen go back along the path. And Macken I want you to look up that way.

He turned to the stranger and looked at his small mouth, teeth canting and crooked like ragged gravestones and the pair of ears on him unfit for a man. Let's go see where it was that you met him.

The man led the way and Faller followed and he told the man to hold up and he lit his pipe and then he resumed walking. They met the river and Faller got down on his haunches for a moment and then he stood up. There's something of the rat about man isn't there? he said.

The stranger looked at him curdled, a dumb face that spoke he didn't know what to say.

Faller smiled. The rat, he said. Scuttles about in filth. Nosing in holes and hovels. Scavenging for scraps. Bearing disease. And always feeding. Always breeding. Can't stop breeding don't you agree?

He sucked on his pipe and realized it had gone out and he took out a box of matches and relit it.

You feel the urge yourself don't you? The urge to fuck, even that upon which nature has decreed should be otherwise.

The stranger was toeing the mud by the riverbank avoiding the man's strange gaze.

I donny know mister what ye mean.

Oh sure you do.

Faller stared at the man as if waiting on his words and the man said nothing and then Faller continued to speak. Man loves the water just like the rat. Not his natural home you see yet man will always be drawn to the water. It's in his instinct.

The stranger turned as if to leave but found himself held by the man's odd smiling address.

Have you ever watched a rat swim in water?

Faller stared at the stranger who squirmed under his gaze with bewilderment and then Faller reached out, grabbed him by the neck and began to drag him.

You would think it had been born to it. The rat. But it's not, you know. And yet put the rat in the open sea and it will tread water for three days they say. I have read that a rat can hold its breath underwater for a quarter-hour.

The man flailed and Faller stopped at the river and looked towards the tarry pool.

Yes indeed, he said. The rat has an instinct for water.

———

HE HAD WATCHED THE MEN go three ways and sat hunkered wondering what to do. Fuck it, he said. He stood up and ran low towards the horses. The animals were strong and glossy and he smoothed the sable flank of one of them as he began to untie the reins from the tree.

The first knot fell like silk and the second with hardly any working at all, and he began shooing away both horses, go on, get, get away with yez to fuck, hissing through his teeth and he went to work untying the third for himself when he turned and saw the girl was watching.

He looked at her with pleading eyes and she said not a word and they stood there a moment staring and then she opened her mouth and began to shout. He's here so he is he's here.

Coyle ran to her and struck her in the face with the flat of his hand and she fell on her knees to the ground. Shut yer bake, he said. Everything was still in that moment but for the drizzle murmuring quietly to itself and he looked at the paths the three men had taken and he saw the horses had begun to wander and then he was away from her, fleeing through the trees.

Brushwood exploding under his feet as he ran, stumbling briefly as he tripped over snaking roots, and the land wobbled as he caught himself and kept running. His breath pounding in his chest and then he saw the fleeting shape of another coming angled towards him. He sensed the man drawing close, too close now to get away, and he pulled himself to a stop fast by a tree. The oncoming rush of feet and the forest floor crackling and the bellowing breaths of the man before Coyle, ready for him, lurched out unseen. He took the other sideways to the ground and they fell separated. They stood up eye to eye, warped and wheezing. He saw the startle in Gillen's hazel eyes. No more than eighteen. I'll have to learn him.

He went to him with his fists. The kid fumbling at the flintlock in his belt and Coyle swung and missed and the youngster instead drove his head into Coyle's chest, forced fingers into an eye socket. Coyle recoiled in pain and he drove a knee to the other man's groin and the youngster went down groaning. Coyle stood panting, his hands on his hips and then he saw clearly the gun, the youngster fumbling to unhook it from his belt and he saw a stick on the ground carbon and ragged like lightning that had burned itself out of the sky and he had it in his hands and swung it. The stick made good with the youngster's jaw, broke off his face half rotten, and the gun and the man went down. Coyle sprung on him, took a hold of the gun and flung it, began hitting him in the face and the other weakened beneath him, a rapt fury as Coyle kept fighting, and then his eyes seized upon a rock and he reached for it with both hands and lifted it. He held the rock suspended in the air and then he saw the other man's eyes, an intensity of living in them, the sheer fright, and he stopped and threw the rock away from him. He got off the youngster and stood.

Go on get up.

He offered his hand. The youngster stood unsteady and his hands were shaking and Coyle rubbed his raw red eye and he glanced about for his hat. Who are ye? he said.

Sheamy Gillen.

Gimme your coat Gillen.

The man took it off and handed it over and Coyle sleeved the jacket. Your hat too. They stood there looking at each other with no sound but for the ragged shears of their breathing and Coyle looked back through the trees over his shoulder. Let me off now on my own, he said. I mean it. Tell him I'm gone another way.

He turned to go but Gillen called out for him to wait, his voice strangely quiet, and Coyle turned around and saw the man's face was earnest.

I canny do that, he said. He's gonna find you. It's like he knows the smell of yer blood.

THE LITHE FIGURE OF FALLER seen quickly from the trees and then he was in the clearing. He saw the girl where she stood and he did not stop but followed with his eyes the direction of her pointing finger. She watched him disappear as quickly as he came and she stood a moment and looked down the forest path towards the river. The child toddled out of the house wearing a look of confusion and he pulled at her leg and she pushed him away and the child went away sulking. He stopped

by the door and snatched a snow kitten by the nape and
when the animal scratched him he cried. He threw the
animal against the wall and the cat righted itself in landing and bolted into the scrub and the girl watched the
scene and then turned towards the forest to see the one-
eyed man dashing through the trees.

She went into the house and did not know what to
do and she went outside and kicked about and then
Faller emerged with Gillen and Macken behind him, the
youngster's shoulders stooped and he was holding in his
hand his bruised face. Faller stopped and looked about.
Where are my horses?

The girl seized, pointed, muttered something fright-
ened. Faller glared. He turned and took Macken with
him to find the horses. Gillen stood there awkward. Can
I get a wee drink of water?

The girl went inside and came out with a cup. Her
hand was shaking. Gillen looked at her. It'll be alright.

Faller and Macken returned with the two horses.
Gillen climbed up slow on his and Faller looked at him
and turned towards Macken. Give him your oilskin, he
said.

Macken's face pussed. I need mine.

Faller stared and Macken shrugged and took off his
coat and handed it up to Gillen. Faller mounted his
horse and ignored the girl who was now standing beside
him. Where is he? she said. Where's me father?

Faller indicated to the others with a nod of his head
and Macken saddled up and the girl pulled at Faller's

boot and asked him again. What did you do with him? Macken and Gillen turned around to look at Faller. He gave the girl a sharp kick and she stumbled onto her hind and then she sat on her sit-bones looking up at him. Faller stared at her in derision. Mamzer, he said. He kicked his heels to the flanks of his horse and the riders moved out.

THE MURMUR OF WATER and he followed till near he came upon the bloom. Brushwood hazed with luminous light then fields of tubular blue. The bluebells stood head-bowed as if quietly mourning their own quick passing or the memory that came as he kicked through their beauty of a time when to see them was small heaven itself.

He found the river and bent to the water and saw his face ripply on the surface. He's tracking me so he is. I can feel it. He scooped water into his hands and drank and then he took off his boots and stepped into the river. The stream flowing against him and foaming around his knees and he waded his way through it. He figured a distance of about a furlong and then he crossed to the other bank and set off at a run near steady. A couple of wee miles just. I canny do more than that. He stopped exhausted where water pooled darkly and foamed over rocks. Across the river he saw a brae thick with gorse. He forded gleaming stones and stepped softly onto the bank, stood dripping and shook the water off him and rebooted and climbed up the hill careful not to leave a track. The gorse was flowered golden and he peered into its thorny embrace, then lowered himself prone and reversed into it. Just enough space for his body and no more, the chamber smelling of earth and musk and the flowers wafting sweet and he lay and closed his eyes.

THE DAY SAT GRAY, all quiet but for the river sleek and ceaseless. He dozed awhile and spent moments coughing, loud enough he figured for him to be heard down below, and he sat a mean hour watching till he saw the shapes of his pursuers appear in file along the other side. Faller in the lead and they seemed in no hurry and the men came to a stop a short distance away and dismounted.

He watched Faller stand by his own and Macken begin talking to him while Gillen stood by his horse. Macken took Faller's water flask from his saddlebag and called to Gillen and threw it towards him. Gillen picked it up and went to the water and filled it and handed it back. Faller went to his horse and fished into his saddlebag and took out his own bottle, drank from it and when it was empty he handed it to Macken who turned and threw it to Gillen. The youngster picked up the flask and threw it back at him and Macken picked it up and stormed over to him and grabbed Gillen by the shirt. The men began tussling and Coyle heard Faller shout for them to stop and Macken went to the water and filled the bottle while Gillen went and sat cross-legged beside his horse.

Coyle watched Faller sit down on the ground and fill his pipe. Balls of blue smoke circled into the air and then Faller alighted his gaze on the hill, kept it there as if in wondering, and Coyle froze and he figured their gaze was met for a good minute but for the screening of the gorse. Go on will ye to fuck.

Faller stood up and began knocking his pipe on a rock and slowly he mounted his horse. He fixed his hat and spoke to the men and Coyle leaned on his breath till the three men rode away.

HE LAY DOWN TO SLEEP in the keep of a tree, wrapped in the comfort of dusk. When he awoke the world was flat and dark and he did not recall what he had dreamed. His teeth were chattering and his stomach rumbled and he wrapped his arms about himself and began walking. The light of the moon skipped moodily between the clouds and when it shone clear it cast a deep shade of blue. In the shadows of fields he sensed the startle of livestock, heard the wary padding of feet away from his motion. He climbed over a ditch that scratched at his legs and fielded stinging nettles and he followed blind a winding road. Against the sky he saw the darker shape of a house barely seen and walked up the brae towards it and circled listening for dogs. The place was silent and there was no outbuilding to see so he walked on not wanting to disturb.

The land leveled around him. Far off to his right he saw a speck of light fattening slowly in the darkness and he figured it for a person with a lantern. He stood and waited till it crossed far off in front of him. The light a blear fighting the dark expanse and he sat watching until the light disappeared, its bearer swallowed whole by an oblivion, and he set off again.

He found a track that rose towards a house and he walked up the verge and went around the back where he came upon the smell of cooped chickens. He found their rough nest under a low wooden roof and felt about for a door. Birds fluttered furiously when he crawled his way in but settled just as soon and he lay down on the straw amongst the droppings and the flies and the molted feathers and he felt warm.

NOT YET MORNING and he was up. The day uncalled by cockerel and he rummaged for eggs in the silver-purpled light, shucked their insides out silken and raw and he filled his pockets with whatever eggs were left and went outside and met the lopsided gaze of a dog. The animal looked at him with liking and he scratched its grayed ears and asked it how far away he was now from Buncrana and the dog looked at him and then answered to his hand with a wet stubbled lick. He began again his journey and the dog followed him for some time listening to his talk. I wonder what you'd do if you were in my place. I'll bet you'd hang about wouldn't ye, bite the problem till the end. A more noble creature you are.

The dog circled the air with its tail and began to nose the side of the road, found a trail and followed it.

I shoulda been born a dog.

He stayed away from the road, canny risk it, and he cut through fields and he avoided a short shower of rain under a tree. He met no eyes and no eyes fell upon him though only so much he could see and he walked till the land slumped bleakly in front of him and he came upon the moss. Scabbing of black amidst brown weave of heather and he trudged on, the blanket rolled in his hand, and he passed under the watch of a steep dun hill and again it began to rain. He tightened his hat, pulled tighter his oilskin and followed the cannelure of track that rounded the hill, the weathered groove meandering and pebbled with the droppings of sheep. The rain stopped and the land blushed in the veiling linger of mist. He saw stones fighting swamp and he spied sheep far off on a hill and he eyed all about for a house of some kind and by noon he found one solitary. He followed the path to it, dim smog from a chimney and a cart canting outside, and he went to the door and knocked. There came no answer and he knocked again and he opened the latch and went in. The smell of turf smoke steeped in the walls. No one about and he found the fire dozing under the keep of ashes. He went to it and poked it alive and he looked about for kindling. The fire snatched at the faggots and he put his hands over the heat for a while and just stood.

The second room housed a bed and on the dresser he saw a knife and he ran his finger over the dull rusting blade and he pocketed it. Lucifer matches too and he slurped old stew potted beside the fire after reheating it and then he sat in the chair and closed his eyes.

Dog bark. He awoke and sat up. Listened again and then he stood, the baying reaching from closer now, and he looked about. He took his blanket and went to the door and slivered it. No one about yet and he opened it wider and slipped outside and closed the door behind him. He took another look and saw the advance party, black dog drumming up the path from the hill.

THE SHEEP SCATTERED from his flailing arms when he went after them. He chased after one and then another that nimbled around a rock and he fixed on one that was slower and went after it, his feet squelching in the black ooze and the animal veering about. He came up to it and grabbed hold of it and he wrested it by the neck and took it to the ground. It lay panting and unblinking and he pulled the knife from his pocket and put it to the animal's throat, began to talk to it in whisperings, there she goes girl not so bad, as the flesh resisted the blunt advances of the knife and then yielded to it and the animal buckled and calmed. He stayed whispering to it like it was a lover as its blood soaked the sedge and drained into the wet earth, the sheep's eyes glassing till finally unseeing he let it fall limp.

He took the knife and began to cut the fleece, scored it around the hoofs and rolled his knuckles between wool and flesh until he had the fleece tubed inverse to the neck. He took the front legs and broke them and then he cut them off and he twisted the head and cut at it until the tendons stretched like they were holding on to some kind of form of the life it once held and then it came free and he put the fleece on the ground and cut the head out of it. The carcass lay violet and still bore heat and he hacked at its midsection and cut the loin out of it and laid it on the grass. He bent to the remains, dragged it and he picked it up and slung it into sludge behind a bunch of heather and he bent and wiped his hands on the heather.

Sullen sky coming down to meet the land and he walked with the fleece around his neck and the meat in his hand and he found the makings of a cave, a rock inviolate against the wearing of the rains and a shelf leaning out to lid the place. He lit a fire that shook yellowing into the blue light and he fixed some sticks upon it. He cooked the meat and ate the charred flesh and finished the last egg and he took the fleece and climbed into the pelted tubing, lay against the shoulder of slanting stone and cursed the rain cunting down when it came.

———————

THE CUTTER WAS CURLED dozing under a sack when the cart groaned to a halt. He heard a voice low in exchange with his brother and then the cart sagged and sprung with new weight and squealed slowly back to life. He heeled the boards with his feet and groaned and lifted the sack to peer at the stranger, pangs of spangled light on his eyes, and he saw a man backturned and then he lay back under the sack.

He awoke some time later and lifted the bag off his face and sat up. The man was sitting sideways with his head wrapped in a blanket, his knees under his chin. The Cutter reached across for a brown bottle by his side and uncorked it with his teeth and drank. He watched the man and then drank some more and he watched the stranger again. He stretched out his leg and tapped the man's elbow with his foot. The man did not stir and he kicked him again and the man whipped off the blanket and glared. The Cutter gave him a big smile then proffered the bottle. The man looked at him darkly then reached out and took a hold of it and he took a slug and his chest seized up and he spat out the contents. The man wiped his mouth to The Cutter's wheezing laugh and handed the bottle back. The Cutter looked at the man's face all bruised and scuffed and his eyes bloodshot and he giggled. You from Ballymagan?

The man shrugged. I donny know where that is.

The Cutter wheezed giddily. You were just in it. Where ye got on. What's yer name?

Coyle.

Call me The Cutter. And this here's Mr. Whiskey.

You're up early, the pair of yez.

The Cutter sucked a long slug and his mouth made a pop leaving the bottle. The dog that bit the hole off ye, he said.

Coyle watched the man curl fetal, black feet poking out from under the sack, a bag and boots by his head. He eyed the landscape in the wan sun, the land dimpled and degged with sprouting color, their passing met by blank bovine stares from huddled herds and he stared idly back. They trundled through townlands indifferent to their passing though still he watched wary and low, the blanket shawled about his head. These settlements seemed thrown into being, haphazard upon the land with their white walls clad in smokedirt and peopled with pigs and the deadstone stares of old women in shawls.

The Cutter was still asleep when it began to rain, a drizzle tentative at first as if it were feeling its way about and then with certainty it began to thicken. The Cutter sat up and pulled the sack over his head and he motioned for Coyle to join him and Coyle took the blanket off his head and balled it and sidled alongside him under the sack.

You for Derry too? The Cutter asked.

Might be.

Make up your mind sir.

They watched the wagging road fall away from them and saw out the rain and when Coyle began to cough violently into his hand The Cutter said nothing but patted the man on the back and told him to swig good from the bottle.

The rolling of the rig put The Cutter into a doze and when he awoke later he saw that Coyle was gone. His brother's voice wroth behind him and the world covered in fog. Across the back of Inishowen they had traveled and now they were alongside the Foyle. The sound of water muted on the lough and he sat himself alongside his brother and peered his eyes onto the disappearing road.

THE CUTTER SAW the black door of the Derry quays tavern and pushed in. Skeletal hands on a mantel clock pointed to half past two and the place full to near-riot. The tavern was dank, a stretch of light weak from a window and one man working the bar to myriad calls for his attention. Tobacco smoke hung shiftless in the air as if it had nowhere to move, the air already laden with the sweat of bodies fresh and the odor of others long past still reeking and in the far corner a door fanned open and shut wafting stale piss. Drinkers were squeezed in lines down benches and their belongings and barrels were piled by the door.

The Cutter got himself a drink and pushed his way through the room with a cup of beer over his head till he came to the back. He saw the edge of a bench and a young man on the end and he saw there was room and he asked the man to push up. The man no more than a boy, wisp of beard and a face that was stingy and narrow as a horse, and he acted as if he did not hear him. The Cutter nudged him and smiled and asked him again to push up but the man supped from his cup and turned his head away from him. A draining smile on The Cutter's lips and he asked the youngster again to move and when he got no response he turned and walked away and then he stopped. He turned and walked back and elbowed his weight onto the seat. Plenty of room, he said and the youngster tipped sideways first and then leaped up from the bench and pulled a knife. The Cutter leaned backwards with his arms out wide and the drinkers around them stood up. Hold on there horsey, he said. The kid cut the air in warning with the blade and was interrupted fast by another who took him by the collar and heaved him back onto the seat putting apologetic words in his ear. The man then turned and offered a hand to The Cutter who stood glowering at the youngster and who turned his attention to his beer pooled and dripping off the table. The man before him with the same face as the knifeman but thicker with age and bearded. Sam Tea's the name and you've just met me brother. Apologies for the way he's acting.

All he had to do was push up.

The man waved his hand as if to dismiss the incident and he put it to The Cutter to shake. The Cutter looked at the hand before him and took it reluctantly and nodded towards his empty cup. Sam prodded his brother and pointed to the empty drinks. In the palm of his hand he danced a few coins. Go on, he said. The youngster went scowling to the bar.

Sam turned to The Cutter and nodded towards his brother. He's half soused so he is and he donny speak so I do the talking for the both of us.

The Cutter sat down. Looks to me like The Mute hears fine rightly.

He hears what he wants to hear.

The Mute arrived back and slapped three beers on the table and sat with his shoulder turned.

Are you for sailing? Sam asked.

The Cutter smiled. Was. Some fog out there.

Across the table a gray-bearded man groused dead-eyed about the weather and the delays it had caused and the cost of a night's lodgings to another who sat half listening, his eyes watery, smiling dumbly over fat glistening lips.

THE FURL AND GRASP of fog and then the road shortened before him. He followed till it met the Foyle and the road along the shore to Derry. Took him a while to realize he knew it. That one trip before with Jim. His brother's laughter. That time they took a cart to Derry to flog a heap of spuds. A battered old horse they borrowed without asking. Must have been just fourteen. My poor brother. And he saw before him the rock of his jaw and the fierce living in his eyes.

The air damp and the sea sullen behind mist. A silence unearthly but for his own footsteps and when he heard the cart coming behind him it was nearly on top of him and he watched the driver well-dressed trundle past his greeting hand. The next one he stopped, heard it coming sooner—an old horse driven by an old man with no words to say but for a tilt of his sandstone head to get on up and Coyle did so and sat behind grateful. He wrapped himself in the blanket and when they neared the walled city the old man stopped and motioned with his head towards his turning and Coyle squeezed the man's shoulder in thanks. He hopped over the side and watched the old man and the horse disappear into the mist like an apparition from his mind that ceased to be.

The start of the city marked by slack-shouldered buildings dim in the fog and he found the streets veiled and lifeless. Evening thickened and he buttoned his coat and adjusted his eyes to the gloom. He followed the road till he was on the quays and he saw the vague shape of the walls rising behind it, the fog lingering upon packet ships fixed lifeless to the docks, the water unheard and the ships silent but for the soughing of their beams. He neared a vessel and saw the figures of sailors smoking on deck, the strangled echoes of one of them laughing while beneath them shone candlelight from a lone berth window.

A redbrick warehouse rose like standing shadow and he saw figures ghosting the mist, people huddling over the flames of barrel fires that danced dimly about the water's edge. He walked among them and saw they were ship passengers not yet departed, their faces looming white and ragged out of the fog, countenances long and few were the words from their mouths. He saw a shawled woman sitting on her belongings and a child on a breast that hung limp and another child sitting nearby and he saw that they were alone. Men sat in circles, idle and heaped with drunken faces and he heard them talking in flat voices or there was no talk at all and he saw children sitting tired as if the fog had sapped them of their vitality.

Gulls hee-hawed in the half-strangled sky and someone came towards him, pulled at his arm and began talking to him, and he saw it was a woman, a face wretched and toothless as she slurred her words whiskey reeking and held a hand out to him in begging. He walked across the quays towards the town rising above him, the cold crawling under his skin, and he stopped to cough and sat down on a wall. The countenance of a man sitting on a sided barrel and he watched him turn towards him, the flesh on his face hollowed to the bone and vicious-looking and Coyle met his stare and the man turned away.

He watched a boy scavenge in the gloom with slant-eyed dogs circling curious, their coats knotted and their tails alert. The boy struggled with a plank of old wood and another boy came a good head taller and he pushed the smaller boy away from the find taking the wood for himself. The small boy fought back with his head tucked into his shoulders and the dogs giddied around them. Coyle watched a man stride over, strike the taller boy on the back of the head and the boy crab away sideways. The man bent to the wood and lifted it to his shoulder and walked off with it.

The cold began to gnaw and his feet were numb in his boots. He blew into his hands and made towards a small fire. He walked past the shape of a man curled on the ground, a coat beneath his body and the man asleep or drunk or both, his hand tight around the neck of a bag with his belongings, and he found at the fire a man and a woman and a heap of children silent. He asked if he could borrow some heat and the woman said surely and they created a gap and let him sit in. The children nursed potatoes on sticks blackening over the flames and the man and the woman were eating quietly. The woman looked at him with dark eyes and smiled with long lips while the man beside her nodded to him, his face hidden beneath a low-pulled cap.

Coyle got down on his haunches and leaned into the heat, the fire scalding the palms of his hands and he rubbed them together. He started coughing and when he finished the woman reached over to one of the children and took the skewered potato from his hand and passed it to the stranger. The child grumbled and the man passed his own stick to the boy and Coyle looked at her and thanked her. When it was cooked he began to eat it, steam bursting the skin and the potato flesh dancing hot in his mouth. The fire began to go out and Coyle offered to help find wood and he left with the man and they walked towards the buildings. Coyle asked him if they were for sleeping outside and the man said they didn't figure on the boat being kept by the fog and he said they'd have to make do like everybody else. They rummaged around the backs of the buildings and broke up some boxes and heaped the wood in their arms and took it back to the fire.

Some of the children began to sleep and Coyle coughed long and deep into his arm and the woman leaned into the man and spoke to him and when Coyle was finished the man asked him if he was alright.

He spoke quietly. I'll do.

The woman spoke up. You be careful. You should find some way indoors tonight.

He looked up at her, tried to see her eyes. I'll be alright. Tis just a cough. I've heard worse so I have.

Maybe so. But I mind my sister had a cough like that.

Coyle said nothing and the woman continued unbidden.

You remember the freeze. Ten year ago. It came in January and it didn't lift till February and everything was buried beneath it. It went up to the knees in some places and you could hardly walk for all the snow and the cold about ye and we couldna harvest a thing.

The man beside her ayed in agreement.

We burned all the fuel we had in that month alone and we sat there indoors, with the father cursing the cold and the idle field outside and him sitting about inside, cursing the weans for there was a load of us. Then one day, it was about three weeks after it started, there was the hint of a thaw—everything started to melt a wee bit and I remember watching the ground begin to slush and the father sent us all out and we started rooting whatever we could get that wasn't ruined in the hard ground.

The woman stopped talking and looked to a small girl who was tugging on her mother's shawl. The mother took the girl in her arm and wiped the girl's runny nose with the sleeve of her smock. Coyle looked around the fire at the children. Shadows darkening their small sleeping faces. One boy awake and he was listening to his mother's story. Go on with your story, he said.

My sister was the biggest of us all, the woman said. Anne was near twenty and I was fourteen. We were freezing and I remember my hands were blue and John, my wee brother, he was a stubborn git. He said damn the work and went to go back inside and my father dropped him with his fist in the field.

We stayed out for hours and then the rain began to freeze and then it started snowing again and the father he paid no attention but Anne told him to look at us and then he told us to go back in but the sister, he told her to stay, and she never said a word of complaining. Later she nearly sat on the fire for need of warmth and the next morning she wouldna get up outta bed with the coughing.

It was thawing a wee bit that day too and the father

he made her get up again and she wasn't fit for it and she told him so but he gave her a box on the side of the head and pulled her out of the bed. She went back out to the field with the rest of us and she was wheezing and coughing and the hands were dark blue again from the cold and it only got worse.

That night the father cursed her high and low, saying what kind of daughter had he brought her up to be and him having no money for a doctor, so we moved her by the fire and we tended to her. It was only when she got much worse, it were late one night, and she was keeping us all awake and we sat around her, she was in a wild fever and she was wheezing badly and she was coughing like it would never stop and the father, he began cursing and he went out and we heard him fixing up the horse and cursing at it and when he came back a few hours later he had the doctor with him.

It was the first time we'd laid eyes on a doctor. He seemed very small for we thought he'd be tall and he didn't say a word but he tapped the sister's chest and he listened to her heart and he put his head to her chest again and we searched his face but it wasn't revealing anything so it wasn't and he didn't even look at any of us. John hiding behind me and then the doctor went by the door and he put on his coat and hat and he spoke to the father but we couldna hear what he said because they were talking in low voices but we saw him nodding his head and we didn't know what he meant by that but later that morning when it got bright anyhow she were dead and the father he died too the year after.

The woman pulled the girl close to her and rubbed a hand through her hair. In his mind Coyle began figuring the best time to go south out of Derry and where to go after that and how long he'd be in hiding. And he saw in his mind images of how he'd get things sorted out. Get back and fix what's left to be fixing. He took hold of the ribbon in his pocket and rubbed it between finger and thumb and the woman saw him with it and he closed his hand around it when she saw him.

So anyways, she said. That's all I'm saying.

THE EVENING WAS MEASURED in cups of beer. The Cutter stood soused to the bar and he saw two men push through, one of them towering above all others and the other man behind him with only one eye. He looked at them and then turned away, something about the manner in which the tall man carried himself, and his way of taking in the face of every man in the room.

He watched the pair go to the counter and the tall man take off his stovepipe hat and put it on the bar. The barman pulled down a bottle of brandy and a bottle of port and poured them into a glass and gave it to the tall man who took the mixture and went over to the fire with the contents swirling. He bent and lifted a poker black-nosed from a bucket and placed it in the burning turf. He waited and took it out glowing. He put it near his lips and blew the dust off it and the steel brightened at the attention of his breath and then he placed it in the drink. The glass began to smoke and the man put the poker back down and shook the mixture and drank.

So COLD HE WAS and his guard dropped low and he braced to enter a tavern. He strolled sober-eyed till he had two unguarded mugs in each hand and he squatted by the fire and drank them. Warmth fired his belly and his head began to ease and he was joined by another man who stood squat-legged and stuffed into his trousers and was too drunk to talk. The man stood with his eyes closed while resting a hand onto the air in front of him as if to steady himself.

Coyle emptied the mugs and got up and went outside and found another tavern. He stood at the crowded counter casual among inebriates and he watched them drinking and he took his chances, a glass untended on a table and he curled his palm around it and when he turned around he knew he was exposed. Above the din rose a voice indignant and then a man quick-standing but Coyle was already gone.

He flitted the shadows that rested their backs upon the doorways and he skulked beneath the gaze of women who solicited him, come here to me you they said, their cheeks a brazen red and their bodies lolling in come-hither affection. Men tumbled from taverns and he sought refuge away from them cramped and bone-weary in a doorway blanketed dark, the smell of piss in the air hung with the voices clattering from the Cowbog, song or shouting they were up to it was hard to tell for singer and shouter approached all the same, and he listened to them barrack their way up the street and watched them kick past him and when a young couple came by and slipped giggling and groping in beside him, they did not see him get up and walk sullen to anyplace else, tired and terribly alone and the streets quietening down around him.

HE FOLLOWED THE MAN. Watched him hang first on the jambs of a tavern door circling the cobbles with his feet. And then the man humped himself heavy into the night dragging an old suitcase behind him. Well-dressed so he was and his face was curlicued with two gray whiskers that rose up near to meet his eyes. He pushed up the street as if heaving weight invisible before him. Coyle heard him wheeze and giggle and listened to the slow plod of his feet.

Gas lamps licked long shadows on the street. The man staggered and stalled and Coyle stepped back to wait against a wall, watched the man fumbling for something in his pocket and saw it was a handkerchief. The man put it to his nose and horned it twice and he leaned forward and began to walk and drag his belongings. He launched loudly into song but the words fell dead from the air as if he could not support them on his own, needed the accompaniment but found none, and he halted again for breath and leaned a hand against a wall. Like this they traveled on the barren street, stopping and starting and Coyle waiting each time behind him, following now behind him in the middle of the street until he became more certain of the idea within himself.

A lane leaned off right and the man turned to take it and he stopped again and dropped his case and stood legs apart, a pool of piss beginning to form at his feet, the urine forking then weaving into a confluence as it trickled down the hill to where Coyle was running upwards towards him now, coming at him sideways with a shoulder that toppled the man off his feet. The man hit the ground heavy on his side and a rasp of air left his lungs and Coyle rolled him over. No word of protest from the man but a low groan, the fetor of booze and sour sweat, and Coyle could not look the man in the face. He reached into the pockets and found a wallet and he took the notes inside and poured out the coins and he paused and put a single note back in the wallet and put it back into the coat and he looked around and then he stood and stole down the street.

He turned a corner, no idea where he was going but to find someplace to sleep. He heard the echo of footsteps behind him and onwards he walked, heard the steps continue behind him and he stopped to wait by a door. The steps died off and he started out again and then he heard them continue. He put his hand into his jacket and tightened a hand around the small bundle of notes and then he stopped and stood in front of the closed front of a shop and he waited. The shape of a boy appeared on the street. Eyes like a cornered rat. Coyle looked at him as he went past and the boy then stopped and turned and stood peering. Coyle looked back at him.

I seen what you done, the boy said.

Coyle pulled his hands out of his pocket.

You didn't see nothing. Get to fuck.

I did. That man on the ground.

I done nothing so I did.

Aye you did and I seen it.

Coyle watched the boy and let his words hang in the air and then he coughed into his arm.

Get away before you make yourself some trouble. I've a pain in me chest and a pain in me head. I'm not in the mood for your shite.

The boy rubbed his nose with the back of his hand and then he took a step closer, his rat eyes peering.

Gimme some.

I'll give you a lug and that'll be the height of it.

I'll tell so I will.

Coyle laughed. Who are you going to tell at this hour of the night?

There's people so there is.

Listen wee fella. I donny want to hurt you so I don't.

The boy was silent and Coyle stepped out of the doorway and the boy took a step back. Coyle walked past him and proceeded up the street. He wandered aimless with nothing now in his mind but sleep, and then he heard the boy was still following and he turned slowly and sighed. Hungry as I am. He waited for him and looked the kid in the face, saw the hard stare of hunger, and he dipped a hand in his pocket and took hold of a coin and threw it back down the street.

Go on, he said.

THE SNUFFLE OF A HORSE and the air kissed him cold and he tried to rub his body, stretched out his legs but found he could hardly move, his limbs dead to the world, and when he opened his eyes it seemed to be early morning, and he saw Jim beside him on a bale, his body robed in shadow but for the fierce gaze of his eyes and Coyle looked at him and he went to speak but he could not find the words and he fought against himself and when he found the power the words were strange in his mouth, sounded like the strangled words of some animal strange to him and they were not what he wanted to say and Jim looked at him sadly and lowered his head and when he spoke Coyle could not hear the words for they were not the words of his brother at all and by then they sounded far away.

The splash of water slapping onto hard ground and then he awoke. The shed lit by morning sun, web-weave on the ceiling and a horse standing placid. The barn doors were opened wide to the morning and he saw the world was still clad with fog. The air alive with the din and dance of the city in this new day and his chest tickled and he started to cough into his sleeve.

He heard steps outside and he tried to stop his coughing and then a figure appeared out of the mist. The nebulous form of a short man took solidity before him, a bucket in each hand, and the man put them down on the ground when he saw Coyle. Would you looky here, he said.

Coyle looked at him and the man scratched his head. Come here Martin and look at that. The man pointed. Another man loomed into shape and put down his pails and peered inside and the two men stood looking at the man covered in straw. Coyle stood up. Sorry to bother ye, he said. I didn't mean any harm so I didn't.

The man slung his thumb backwards into the air and then shook his head and smiled. Go on, get.

MACKEN WAS SITTING on his own spooning porridge downstairs in the tavern when Gillen shoved his bowl alongside him. Morning, he said. Macken grunted. Gillen pointed his finger towards the ceiling and lowered his voice to a whisper. How do you figure Faller knows where to find him?

Macken spooned more porridge then picked up a cup and slugged down the remainder of the tea. He just does.

Gillen watched him. I mean, there's loads a places any man running could go to.

Macken licked the spoon then shoved the bowl away from him and stood up. He put on his jacket without looking at the other man and spoke then as he was leaving the table. There's two ways he can run, he said. He can get out of here by catching a sailing or he can leave the city by going south through Bishop's Gate where I'll be waiting for him. Any man serious about getting away wouldn't bother to do anything else.

He began walking towards the door when Gillen called out after him. Hey, he said.

Macken stopped and half turned. What?

I know what happened to your eye.

Go an fuck off.

I heard the rumors about what you were doing with that man.

Gillen laughed and shimmied his hips mockingly at him and Macken snapped his body around stunned and pulled a knife. I'm sick of your shite, he said. He went towards the youngster and Gillen ran around the other side of the table and made a leap for the stairs.

FALLER'S WEAPON SAT fat on the table like some ornate beast that had winged down obscure, the flesh of both barrels burnished bright and detailed with exotic flourishes while the wood stock was a consortium of animal carvings, eyes and tails and mouths engorging each

89

other so that it looked like some pageant of evil was unfolding. The end of the grip led to a beast's head, some kind of creature mythic with fangs poised as if to devour the hand of the shooter.

Gillen sat in the room above the tavern watching him take apart the gun. The room was sparsely furnished but for two beds, a bunk and a single, that took up the other wall. He had seen Faller unholster it and leaned forward to look, a flintlock pistol double-barreled, and he looked at his own gun meager on the bed, a flintlock with a single bore made of plain wood and steel, inferior on all counts not just in style but in substance too. He looked at the double barrels and followed the line to the weapon's firing mechanism, the frizzen curling upwards like the ear of some kind of thing demented, and his gaze trailed till he was looking at the holder of the gun, noticed Faller's deep breathing, a man in concentration or contemplation perhaps, for who was to know whatever it was that man was ever thinking, and then every short while he would lift his head up to look out the greasy window.

Gillen stood up and peered out the window too.

We're for the quays are we? he said.

Faller continued to take apart his gun as if the man beside him never spoke. He unscrewed the plate and removed the frizzen and placed it on the table and he took a cleaning jig and swabbed gently the throat of the gun, working it up and down to remove any powdered residue. He took a brush in his hand and cleaned the weapon's vent hole and wiped the frizzen and he took a can and oiled all the parts. Gillen listened to the man's breathing and the tock of a clock in the hall and he cleared his throat.

What's it like? he said. He wrung his hands and put them back on his lap. To shoot, I mean.

The question hung in the air unanswered and Faller tilted his head to the window and began assembling the gun. Each part was handled with care and attention, the parts lifted orderly from the table and smoothed with long fingers. When the gun was assembled Faller raised the weapon and half-cocked each chamber and he turned around and pointed the business end of the handgun towards Gillen's facc. The young man stared at the weapon's snorting cavities.

You haven't killed a man have you? said Faller. He placed the gun back down on the table.

Gillen slumped back in the chair. I seen it done.

You've seen it done?

Faller removed a bag from a pouch hanging on a chair and put it on the table beside the gun. You're not the kind for it though.

I am so.

You're the kind that panics.

Faller looked at him and his moustache rose up to meet his nose as he smiled. He took from the bag a parcel containing a cartridge box and put it on the table. To be the last thing a man sees before he dies, Faller said. Nothing will make you feel more alive.

How do you mean?

Faller lifted the gun and nosed the barrel towards the ceiling. He bit into a cartridge and poured some powder into the pan and closed the frizzen and poured the remaining gunpowder down the barrel and then held the gun in front of him admiring it.

It's quite a moment, said Faller. To be the sole judge of that person on earth. You meet his eyes and there's an understanding quite like no other.

Gillen's eyes wandered to a dark stain slugged on the wall and he looked upon the thinning fog out the window. In his mind he saw the face of Coyle looming over him and he sucked in his breath. Killing's a dirty business, he said. There's no pleasure in it.

Faller smiled at Gillen. And what would you know?

The younger man fiddled with his hands. Faller took between finger and thumb the ammunition for the gun, two bullets fat and round like marbles. He dropped each one down a barrel and took the ramrod and pushed the bullets down the gun's throat and stood up and stretched his hand around the bulk of the weapon and with a long thumb put each chamber on half-cock. And then he put on his hat.

COYLE WALKED AIMLESS through the city. The ache in his feet something terrible like it was trying real bad so it was to drag a man down into the earth. The fog tearing now into tendrils that exposed the working noises of the city, the clatter from carriage and trap and the barking from men's voices. He put a hand into his pocket for some oats and they sat on his tongue like sawdust. He went to a horse trough and scooped some water quickly into his mouth and ignored the passing stare of a gentleman.

The sun was gaining power over the brume and then it began to rain. He tightened his hat and buttoned his coat and stood in the doorway of a shop. Signs for tobacco surrounded him each side and he watched two women plump and well-dressed join him in front. One of them turned with a wobbling double chin and took a glance at Coyle, appraised him fully for what he was, and he ignored the look and watched vaguely elsewhere. The rain began to stipple the street with stubby thick drops and he heard the door of the shop squeal open to a bell tinkle and close behind him. A man stepped out and looked up and down at the sky and then he blinked with his single eye. Coyle looked up and saw the profile of Macken and his body tensed at the sight, saw the man dally under the awning and pull a newspaper from his pocket and begin to read. Coyle pulled his hat over his eyes and slumped down into the wall as if the building was something he could merge into while Macken stood with Coyle obscured to his limited field of vision. Macken turned the page of the newspaper and folded it and put it close to his face and he put it down and put a hand into his jacket and looked at a timepiece from his pocket. The jowled woman leaned over and asked him the time. Near eleven, he said. He folded his newspaper and put it into his jacket and turned to the two ladies and nodded to them and he left pushing up the street. Coyle lifted himself out of the wall and stood a minute and then he pushed through the ladies and watched Macken disappear. What the fuck, he said. Loud mutterings from one of the women behind him and he turned and walked across the street.

HE WALKED AGAINST THE RAIN, his hat visored against it, and he was wondering what he would do. The road south and there was Macken walking in the direction of it. What the fuck, he said. He shrunk away from the people milling past him, turned for a side street and stopped to cough. It dug into him deep, emptied him out, and he saw Macken's face in his mind, the single-eyed shock of it, and when he stopped his insides were sore.

The rain softened and then stopped and he walked on aimless without certainty where he was for. He walked past a boy leaning on a wall, saw the features of the youth from the night before and quickened his pace and then realized it wasn't him. The boy was chewing from a thick wadge of buttered bread and in the other hand he held an onion and he took bites out of it as if it were an apple. Coyle put his hand into his coat and secured in a fist the cash and he shook the oats loose from his pocket scattering them onto the street.

He walked further on looking for some place discreet to eat. He saw a shop and stopped outside it looking in the window. Loaves of brown-crusted bread. And then he felt an arm reach around him, his neck in a lock as if the intention was to pull him to the ground, and he twisted out of it in alarm. Wild-eyed he looked up. The Cutter stood smiling with his hands on his big-boned hips and then he did a quick dance for him. I was wondering where ye got to, he said. Are ye coming?

Coyle shrugged. Huppidy hah.

He followed watching over his shoulder. The Cutter chatting away saying he was off for some food and a drink and what a wild head he had on him. He followed him towards the Cowbog and into a bar and he cast his eyes nervously about. The place a spill of shadows and half empty. Nothing here to be afraid of. They sat down beside a dancing fire. Two bowls of tripe soup so thick you could stand on it and two cups of beer and The Cutter did all the talking. He giggled to himself as he told his stories, yarns accumulated from the night before that took on magnificent proportion as he told them, stretched out his arms wide as if to demonstrate the realm of them, and when he was done telling he would slap his belly and laugh wholeheartedly. Coyle supped on his cup and saw that it was dirty and he tried hard to listen but found it hard to talk in return and then there was the fact that his entire body was weakening.

———————

An hour or two passed and something not right. His throat tight and a wheezing in his chest. The beer in front of him unwanted and the crowd swelled on top of him, the darkness in the tavern tightening around him and he felt the need to escape. He stood up from the table and turned around. He threw his gaze to the top end of the tavern and there it met the eyes of Faller and their eyes locked, formed a bridge that linked these two men over the heads of all others. And then the man was pushing through the crowd a good head over most of the men, his hands to the shoulders of those that blocked his path, and he made light of them beneath his weight as he shaped his body into a charge. Coyle turned and made for the back door, fumbled at the latch, his hand shaking and the door, it would not open for him, stiff as it was, and he leaned back and gave it a kick and he found himself facing out into a narrow yard where the weather had closed in darkly, rain falling down from a sky that kept on giving, a sky that had never once been the same since the day he was born and for all the days he was not born, yet a sky that had remained exactly the same. And the sound the rain made as it fell to the earth filled up the moment with a kind of peace.

———————

THE CITY ENCLOSED in a tumult of rain. The bustle of the streets quietened down as people sought reprieve, huddled in doorways and under eaves where they cursed the weather or hid beneath the dripping tarpaulins of marketeers. They watched too with suspicion the fleeing figure of Coyle, wondered what kind of trouble he was up to, and no sooner was he gone than they were arrested by the sight of another, a towering man in pursuit hardly running at all it seemed but walking.

Coyle turned upon the butchers' shambles and pushed into the crowd, a runnel of offal gut and blood veining at his feet. A man with a knife stood sharpening it on stone, his cheeks blazing like fresh red chops, and he looked at Coyle, watched him suck on shallow breath as he stood by his stall and then he turned again to his stone. Coyle pressed on, threaded the thin crowd, past the entreaties of butchers and the marbled sarcophagi of hanging carcass meat and went in the direction of Bishop Street towards the gate that would lead him south out of the city. He looked behind him and a carriage swung in front of him and then he saw Macken standing sentry under the archway. Coyle stopped dead in the street, two small boys beside him rolling bottles, and he stared at Macken but the man was nosing a newspaper and Coyle turned on his heels, ran down a narrow street where the bustle of the city took reprieve in its shaded silence and he tried the brass handle of a door and found that it opened into an unlit empty room and he stole inside and stood there.

———————

He watched The Cutter leave the tavern with his head tilted in laughter and he followed him down the street. The rain had worn away the lingering fingers of fog and the sun strode sharply. The Cutter was talking to another man as Coyle stole alongside him, took him by the elbow, come here a minute he said, and steered the man incredulous off the street. The Cutter waved to the other man and he followed Coyle who took frequent watch over his shoulder.

Yer some fella for running off, said The Cutter.

I need yer help.

I can't give you no money.

I need you to get me a ticket for a boat. I'm paying so I am.

Which one?

Any one. The first one that's leaving. Here.

Coyle took out a wad of notes and put a five-pound note into The Cutter's hand. He stood looking at the money. The difference is for yourself. Coyle closed the man's hand around the money. Just go over to one of the agencies and get me a ticket for the first boat that's sailing. I donny care where for.

Where'll I find ye?

By that wooden hut over there.

The Cutter looked at Coyle and tipped his cap. Just for you, he said. Seeing as I know that you're not from

Ballymagan. Hoor of a place. Wouldna do nothin there for nobody.

HE SAT ON A BOX, hiding by the wall of a redbrick warehouse among barrels and boxes, and bunkered down into coughing. His coat was hitched over his head against the slanted rain. The Foyle now divested of fog and the water leaning north like an invitation. He watched a cargo steamer being loaded and launched and then guided by tug upriver. Slug trail of white water and then the boat shrank from sight.

The screeching around him of rats and he saw one brazen before him. It hunched downwards vertical on a barrel to nose at his feet, stretched and straightened with its pelt the color of moss. Black-beaded eyes and earthworm tail and he watched it nosing the dirt and loose grains, the scuffling scratch of claws on boot leather. Are you looking at me queer fella? Man and creature eyed each other for a moment and then the rat was gone.

He watched the Murmod come to life. Saw officials board and the crowd began to swarm around the boat, swallow whole a horse and cart to coalesce into a single knot that hived towards the gangway, cases and casks hitched up over their heads and small children being carried. Everywhere the din of hawkers selling their wares, food and drink and other such comforts, shysters and moneylenders working the crowd and pickpockets quick on their feet.

He guessed an hour go by. Near everyone from the quays on the boat, relatives and friends and who knows what else to clutter the deck and go below to the holds to say their goodbyes and none of them by the looks of it wanting to leave. The bladed rain stopped and he looked up to see a cloud bank burl from near-black to white, the Foyle spangled in new sun. He watched the gulls swoop and plummet the ship's three masts and glide down to rummage the quays. A horse and trap turned around to leave and when it pulled away he saw Faller in its wake. Jesus. He picked him out from the far side of the crowd standing with Gillen, watched him pace up and down and then the crowd moved and his view was blocked. He strained his neck to see. Goddamn ye.

A parting among the bodies and then Coyle saw the back of Faller walking towards a cargo steamer that was being loaded further down the quays. He looked down at his nails, picked the black dirt from under them and he ran his hand down the length of the dull blade in his pocket and sat a while thinking.

GILLEN WATCHED THE disappearing back of Faller, turned and saw to his right the black silhouette of a sailor spidered on a web of halyards. He watched a group of young children disembark from the boat and scatter like leaves in front of a red-eyed woman who turned and stood waving. And then a man protesting was dragged scudding on his heels by two officials off the boat. The man stood on the quays and waved his fist and stood shouting. Crew tarried near the gangway and the Murmod was near ready to depart. And then Gillen saw Coyle coming towards him, the man with his hands in his pockets and his hat and head down low but he knew the cut of him, watched him push through the crowd, the man not lifting his head and making towards the gangway where he was stopped by an official and Gillen looked quickly over his shoulder to see if Faller was watching.

FALLER STOOD AT THE OTHER end of the quays watching stevedores loading a cargo ship. He could see Macken at the other boat. He lit his pipe and sucked on the smoke and looked towards the clotted sky, the clouds an uncertain wash of white, and he sniffed the air, inhaled the smell of hops and heard the squeaking of axle. A cart trundled behind him, a stonemason whistling tunelessly, and as it passed he saw a boy and a girl sitting atop slabs on the back. The boy held the girl's hand on his lap and when he saw Faller he let go of the hand and Faller stared back.

Faller walked over to a sailor and tipped his hat to him, asked him where the ship was going. Glasgow, the man said.

Are you taking any passengers with you?

Not today, the sailor said. Full load of freight.

Faller turned and saw a tramp hunching on a limp towards the pair of them. The sailor saw him too and walked off.

Master. Go on give us some tobacco.

Faller looked at the man, saw gums housing a handful of teeth, eyes wide in supplication and cloth wrapped around damaged-looking feet, and he sucked on his pipe and blew smoke in the man's face. Dance for it, he said.

The man grimaced and blinked.

I said dance.

The tramp's face dropped and the man stood still as if summoning some reserve from tired bones and he turned his head and looked around to the quays behind and looked towards the stevedores and saw that no one was watching. With intake of breath he began to dance, a stiffening stumble that lurched awkward from heel to heel with his arms hooked to his sides, danced with his head locked straight and his eyes on the man who was asking and Faller smiled back down at him and then sucked on his pipe and said put some back into it will you. The tramp took a breath and danced wilder still, danced wincing on a limp, spit on beard, knees unfurling legs that were spindled and spent and the cloth bundles unfolding from his blackened feet, the man hobbling and hurling backwards across the quays with his head thrown to the sky, turning and turning.

Faller turned and walked back to Gillen and found him as he had left him. The ship was fully boarded and a scattered crowd stood waiting for it to depart. He watched sailors reel the Murmod's mooring onto deck and saw them begin to lift the anchor.

He paced back and forth and stopped and turned to Gillen.

No sign of him?

Naw.

Walk back up to the gate and lend that blind bastard your eyes, he said. Gillen turned and began to walk and stole a glance over his shoulder. Faller was putting his pipe in his pocket and stood facing the boat.

Faller walked around taking in the scene in front of him and then he stopped with his hands on his hips. He watched people waving from the quay and he looked at the wooden bridge spanning the Foyle and then he walked towards the crowd. Out in the water, seabirds flurried hungry around a fishing boat. He looked up at the Murmod, watched the paddle-tug take the strain of the ship on its tow rope as the ship slid forward into the waters. He looked again at the faces lined up on the boat, men and women and children, some sodden in emotion and others not sodden or waving at all but standing stone-faced, and then out of the crowd he picked a face, the profile of Coyle walking quickly to get across the deck, and Faller smiled.

THE MEN ASSEMBLED their belongings and left the city on horseback. The sky the color of gunmetal and the rain pressed down upon their sitting trot, beading their oilskins and Faller oblivious to it on his black steed. He rode out north in front of Macken with Gillen lagging behind, the man wearing a purple bruise on his face, and they followed the road for a number of miles. They turned off the road at Glendoagh upon a bridle path and Macken nudged his horse alongside Faller's and asked where they were going.

I have a man to see.

Macken nodded and slipped behind and the group rode on. They sidled a forest that swallowed the light and passed a forge where the beating of anvil pealed like a muted bell. The clanging stopped and a bearded man leaned out on the jambs to watch the backs of the riders.

Lowering sky and the rain fell relentless and then Faller began to slow. He turned to a tapering path beat down by foot and the men rode on behind. Sedge scrunched under horse weight and the land opened to the bog, the encroached horizon of slumping dun hills and then they were riding upon the moss. The peatlands were sheeted in brown and yellow and dotted with the lone whites of sheep. A turf barrow nosed a pool in rotting and they passed patches of heather scalped, opened turf banks slaned like cliffs cut in miniature to a sea of wind-waving moss. To the west a tarn, a brooch of silver around the low neck of a hill. To the north a house isolate and they rode towards it. They met a black-faced ewe that stood stubborn and then skittered out of their way and the house rose into sight and then they were upon it, the place empty and bearded with growth, and then they rode on past it.

To hills beyond they went, Gillen watching sullen the backs of the men. He saw Faller come to a stop and watched him take out his pipe and he caught up with Macken and the pair stopped alongside Faller.

They sat in silence under the banks of sky, in their ears the hiss of rain and the empty whisperings of wind.

Faller lit his pipe, sucked on it and spoke with the pipe hanging in his mouth.

You saw him didn't you? he said.

Gillen looked at Faller whose eyes were fixed ahead upon the wilderness and he looked at Macken whose back was turned towards them. He swallowed and then hitched up his voice.

You asking me?

The youngster's words scattered on the breeze.

Faller spoke. Yes you did. You saw him and you let him board.

The words seized the air around Gillen, tightened the breath in his lungs, and he looked around him.

No man went past me that I didn't see.

The words fell from his mouth, tumbled without the fixative of certainty to fall upon the moss and strew away, a waver in the man's voice belying the truth of what told. The conversation now appeared to be over and Gillen fumbled with the reins on his horse and he began to whistle, an aimless tune of hollow indifference, and Faller sucked on his pipe and sent smoke in long drafts to reach out and encircle entire hills. He looked at Macken and nodded to him and Macken fixed his hat and took hold of the reins and nudged his horse forward to ride on. Gillen sat behind and waited for Faller and saw that he was not yet for moving and Faller turned to him and nodded for him to ride on behind Macken and Gillen kicked his horse forward.

PITTED THE BOG WAS with silver pools of rain that spread like the markings of some beast that prowled its prehistory, the wetlands older than the footfall of man and indifferent to such wanderings. Gillen rode alone midway between the men and took to watching the sky, was watching the great gray swirling banks of it and a chink of light that broke through the heavens to pillar in gold the top of a hill when the bullet from Faller's gun entered the left side of his head, the trajectory of the ball uncoupling half of his face with it to spread upon the bog, the sound of the shot traveling slowly behind to reach ears already dead.

The clatter of shot sent Gillen's animal onto its hind legs, the dead weight of the man slumping harness-caught above the ground. The animal danced nervously then settled and Macken turned around to see the body of his colleague hanging from the horse and he rode over to it and leaned over and spat. Slowly Faller reloaded his gun and reholstered. He looked at Macken.

The fucker took the boat, he said. He nodded to the body.

Feed him to the sheep.

LAST SIGHT OF LAND, a voice said. Coyle followed the others to the deck to see but the ship was enclosed by fog. He had thrown the knife into the sea and watched from on deck the boat push up the Foyle, the sea a slate of gray animated in the rain. He sleeved away his tears. The wee child without me. This is not what I wanted at all.

The air on the deck hung quiet in the snarling murk but for the chatter of sailors at work while the passengers stood in small groups silent. They strained their eyes expectant towards the land just left, this land known lifelong to feet, loam for curling toes, a mass of ground fixed solid to the earth and immutable to mind but for the wearing of memory as relentless as the sea, but there was no shoulder of land to lean on, no buttress of rock, no green-fringed cliff nor sight of fields, just the wash indeterminate of gray, the land, the sea, all sky.

WHEN I WAS WEE GIRL *I heard the story of the riders and I wished with all my heart it werna true. But Mary Crampsey said it was and she knowed everything so she did so I believed her. She said that kind of thing went on years ago, happened to her second cousin who lived up near Binnion, and I used to think all the time about it after that. I'd lie there at night in me bed and if it were a windy night and the window was rattling I'd be afeared it was them coming to get me. Sure I was only a young un then. It took me a long time till I could shake it out of my head. I mean just the thought of it—what would they be for doin with you? I used to wonder but I was afeared to ask anyone and later when I became a grown woman I understood rightly. Knew what it was to a woman that a man could do.*

Mary said they'd come in a gang on their horses and they'd go into your house in the middle of the night and they'd just take you, pick you up over their shoulder and carry you off pillion into the dark. Off you'd be taken to some other parish where you would never be seen by your family again. She said there was one time the riders were caught and that was how she knowed about it. It was that time with her second cousin Peggy Crampsey, now dead so she is—what was it now, oh she got the cough—and she was saved because her father was quick to his wits about it. He was comin home from a wake sluiced with the drink and he found them goin into the house and he kept a huge cudgel of a stick in the yard and he beat the men off her so he did.

When I thought of that story for years after I'd be awfully afeared. To me that was the worst kind of horror. And it was only later I realized what they were up to. There's men who have a need and I know that surely and I know sometimes there's men who donny get married and they got that need carried around with them all stored up. I can understand that they got to do something with it. And not everybody has the kindness in them. So to me it makes some kind of sense. Terrible and all as it is I can understand it, I can see there's a reason for it.

But what I couldna get my mind around was the reason we were being turned out. I asked about afterwards and nobody could tell me anything. Nobody wanted to talk and those that did said nobody knew. We owed nothing so we did and the land was useless to him. And I gotten then to wonder that it must have been something that Coll went and done. And then one time, soon after the second wean was born, I met Wee Paddy Doherty and he told me that I should go find Bridie Butler who kept the big house for the Hamiltons. She had ears for everything he said, and there wasn't nothin that she didn't know. If anybody could tell you, he said, it would be her.

Part II

THE FIRST DAYS PASS AND HE DREAMS DARK, SICKNESS deepening into him, and he lies between two worlds. The eyes of strangers he sees bunked in the shadows and he knows the look of suspicion, knows that a man's sickness is not to be meddled with. He turns throughout the day, days becoming night twisting like a knife and night darkening into some kind of void that puts a hold on time. He lies there buckling in the grasp of it, the world no world now. Sometimes he loses sense of the pain, the vise that clasps tight his chest, the teeth tearing deeper at his lungs. He forgets the weakness that has claimed his body and he drifts sleep-haunted. She comes to visit him but he cannot be sure if she came at all but he talks to her and she feeds him water and mops his brow, she who is his mother and his wife, the cold cloth on his burning forehead, and when he opens his eyes he sees also it is his friend.

He dreams he is in his bed and the fire asleep to find that Hamilton is on top of him, their bodies writhing, and he gulps air panicked in the roaring darkness, the man grappling silently to pin the limbs of his body, a head burrowing into his trunk as if he had the rabid

113

power to break sternum, rip ribs apart, and he's beating against the other man's chest with his fists, hands coiled with murder, the two men in the act of killing and he grasps at Hamilton's throat or pulls at his mouth, a twisted toothy rictus. In the tussle he sees into the man's eyes but they are sightless ghostly orbs and he sees between the weave of the man's hair the perforation of skull, a lacquered rim of dry dark blood and inside the man's head a blackened void beckoning. Disgust drives him to kill the man again and again, pounding him with his fists and he reaches and finds a knife and jags the man's chest with it and another time he is reaching for a hammer and when he is free of him sometimes he looks at the face of the dead man and sees the face of his own brother and sometimes just as he is finished Hamilton rises inexorable to meet him and the two lock all over again.

His breathing is so shallow he thinks it will cease, the architecture surrounding his chest will snap finally and be done, and he trembles with the cold and someone puts another blanket on him but he feels no warmth from it. He feels the chilled hand of a woman on his flaming head and notices the scent of her, dried sweat and biscuit and the whiff of faint perfume and all around the air thick with salt. Sometimes, too, he awakes and his mind is so still he can rise above the calamity in his body and see past the darkness of the hold towards a light, a bulging fish eye he thinks, the light of another world reaching for him where he lies. Sometimes he awakes and he finds himself enclosed in the dim light of this no world at all but for the dancing shadows cast by a shimmering slush lamp.

He hears the men talking but cannot fasten his mind onto their words. There is always talking, the comforting hum, and he cannot understand what they are saying but sometimes he is aware they are talking about him.

What he does not hear are the words of some men, fearful that whatever is eating through him they will wake in their cots with it next, but though they complain there is nothing they can do. Some of the men talk of putting him outside but another speaks up for the sick man and warns them away. The first mate comes down to have a look, his face wind-chiseled and lit by wise blue eyes, and he winces when he comes upon their foul odor. He notes the look in their eyes, their fear and suspicion, and tells them in his estimation that what the man has does not resemble ship fever.

Coyle dreams of his father and his mother and he is ageless and he is a child and he is haunted by the face of his wife. She stares at him with her sloping sad eyes and she asks him if he will be back and he gives her the child and tells her he doesn't know and they are walking on the beach, the damp sand clustered about his toes and the surf foaming and over her eyes her hair is windblown.

He is stirred by the sound of crashing, something colossal, and the edifice around him groans as if lashed in agony, as if it were about to be pulled apart or split from under him, and in the silence that falls between the great sounds of the sea he hears the shouts of men, voices grave and epic. He feels everything slide from under him and he rolls about and is thrown from the bed he lies on and a man comes to the floor and talks to him and holds him still.

He has an idea the man has a boat and he asks him if he can borrow it and the man says nothing and he asks the man again, for he wants to go into the boat now, but the man gives him water and tells him he is on the boat now and not to be worrying and that everything will be alright.

How many days like this he cannot fathom. But then the burden of dreams is lightened and sleep settles easier. For the whole of a day and the whole of a night he sleeps deep and soundless, nothing to disturb him in this new vale of peace. And when he awakens dreamless, his eyes blinking and he has the strength to sit up, he looks out of the hold of the tween decks where he sees the stretching light of an afternoon. And then one by one he sees the faces of the men take shape. A plume of blue pipe smoke, flinty eyes above their bowls, hands busy at cards or mouths quietly talking, and they are sitting on their bunks, some of them staring at him and others insouciant. And he awakens to the smell, the rancid sweat that sticks to the air, stale piss and the fetor of feces, and then a voice, a man with a husky growl, calls out from somewhere in the room.

Hey Cutter. Yer man. He is awake.

THE ATLANTIC. THE HEAVING, swollen eternity of it. He drank it in, became delirious on it. The Murmod's jib jutting off the bow as if to show with pointed finger the direction of their journey but there was no bearing visible and his mind was stricken that first time, the water's reach encircled and so endless that it seemed the world had fallen off some great precipice while he was sick, slipped like a great sheet of ice and was gone.

He watched the endless weaving of the waves and he listened to the sails suck their cheeks in the wind and he walked about the deck, watched women in their huddles and men idle with their hands in their pockets and dark-eyed children flit unwatched. The air stout with smoke. Charcoal fires burned from cabooses on each side of the ship, each terminal surrounded by shabby figures who watched over burning griddle bread and stirabout in smoking pots and their brattling voices stirred with the smoke that circled on the wind and blew back into their faces.

He sat down in the shadow of a man who spooned from a plate of food on his lap. The man was bald with wings of curling gray hair and he nodded his wrinkled brow when he saw Coyle and Coyle nodded back. The man produced from a satchel a piece of food and he unwrapped it and put it to his nose and smelt it.

Smoked fish. As soon as it was on his plate he was en-circled by three boys and they heckled him for some of it, a share of your good fortune they said, their eyes burning, and he ignored their pleas till a dirty paw reached over his spooning hand and made a grab for the fish. The man leaped up and his food tipped to the floor and Coyle exploded laughing. A boy took the fish from the ground and disappeared into the crowd and the man grabbed the boy nearest to him and slung him backward on his lap. He began to beat the child with the flat of his hand and a woman stepped shrill from the caboose and he wouldn't stop till she took a fist of his hair. He stood up, his cheeks burning, and he stared at her in disbelief and then he sat down again muttering.

The Cutter appeared alongside him and he put a hand on his shoulder and laughter shook his great belly. The man glowered and The Cutter sat down heavy-boned beside Coyle. There he is, he said.

Here I am.

The Cutter nodded towards the other man. The wee hellions. They're always at him. Isn't that right Noble? They'll be picking at ye all the way to America.

Noble sat fuming and ignored the digs of The Cutter who was now elbowing Coyle in the ribs.

He keeps to himself but he's alright. A cooper from Fermanagh. You could be worse hey Noble? And how is Inishowen today?

Inishowen?

That's what we call you on account of where you are from—knowing nothing about ye.

I'm alright so I am.

The Cutter took out his pipe and filled it with tobacco. Got any tinder?

Naw.

The Cutter stood up and borrowed a box of matches and lit his pipe and put the matches back in his own pocket. He sucked on the pipe and blew smoke against the sky and then nodded towards it.

Have you noticed yet? he said.

Coyle looked up. The whiteness of the sky and the clouds near invisible against it. The Cutter nodded again.

Birds, he said. I ain't seen any in days.

Coyle smiled and stood up and began to walk about. He watched a small boy with a dirt-streaked face stumble upon the deck. Watched him race on speeding feet and fall tiny among tree-trunk legs. The boy picked himself up again and wandered examining the boards as if they held something mysterious and then he folded his legs and sat down upon them. He began to play with seashells from his pocket, lined them out at his feet into a single row. In the boy he recognized the face of his own child, saw the hands of his daughter testing the shapes of stones, heard the small bundle of her voice, and he turned towards the great void of the sea, his breath held in his chest and he looked out into the distance where time and movement seemed to hold still, where nothing seemed to happen at all, a void bereft of love and pain, a great wash of unmemory held in its ceaseless eternity.

THE CUTTER FINISHED his food and he licked his fingers. We thought you were a goner, he said.

Coyle looked up from his food and then he spooned it into his mouth. The oats thick in his gob while he spoke. Have ye never seen a man sick before?

Aye. But there's rarely a man sick as you who has come out of it.

There's nothing else to do around here but get better. It took me a long while though to figure that out.

There ain't nothing to do around here but get sick.

I've tried that. I donny recommend it.

Across from them two young fellas began play-acting, each taking the other in the grasp of a mock wrestle.

If you see the master's wife you can thank her.

Why's that?

It was she who came to your assistance. The ship's mate keeps track of anyone who is ill. She came down to see you a few times. Gave you drops of some stuff to help you sleep.

I wonder what it was.

She said she didn't think you had the ship fever.

I'm still not right.

You're looking stronger.

It's not on account of the food.

Seven pounds of bread, flour or rice per man each

week and three quarts of water per day. A fine cele-
bration.

The wrestlers began to attract a crowd eager for en-
tertainment. One of them was red-haired and short and
he took the other fella with an ankle trip to the ground.
The wrestlers smiled through clenched teeth and then
the redhead was grabbed by the groin and he howled
and let go his grip. He reached instead for his oppo-
nent's hat and he grabbed it and ran off. The Cutter
stood up to watch and began to laugh and Coyle stood
and watched the action and then he nodded towards a
family that was eating.

I see there's a wise many that brought their own but-
ter and eggs.

Aye. And you didn't bring anything.

Naw.

And why was that?

I was in a wild hurry to get away from that hellhole.

The redhead stood starboard with the hat dangling
over the sea and the other fella reached him and began
to yank at his arm. He pulled the redhead by the ear and
the redhead yelled out and he let go of the hat. Dumbfounded the man watched as his hat sailed on the wind,
rose on a vapor as if taking flight and then decided to
settle on the sea. The crowd rushed forward to gawk
over the edge and they started howling and laughing
and the redhead broke free and ran for below deck.

Coyle looked at the people around him. How many
people on board are there? he said.

I'm guessing about one hundred and fifty or so.

And I see the families keep to themselves.

Aye.

And the women to the women's quarters too.

Well that depends, if you know what I mean.

Coyle cocked a quizzical eyebrow.

Let's just say I'm hearing there's one or two of them that are welcome to a visit.

The Cutter winked and rubbed an invisible coin in his hand and Coyle shook his head and laughed.

And it was you who gave me straw?

I asked about for you.

That was kindly.

What's a man to do?

You could be counting stray birds.

The Cutter smiled. Man is sometimes a more curious thing to watch than beast.

Do you reckon?

Aye. Take you for instance.

What about me?

Well, for one, yer always futtering about with that dirty ribbon. And you look like a man who could be running from something.

Coyle found himself balling his hand and he put the ribbon into his pocket.

And how did you figure that out?

The Cutter just smiled a row of crooked teeth and turned to follow the brawl below deck.

HE TOOK HIS FOOD from the galley and descended the poop ladder singlehandedly below. The low hum of talk in the single men's quarters and he found The Cutter swinging his feet on the top bunk and men on his own bed smoking.

Here he is.

One of the men made to get up but he told him to stay and he sat down on Noble's bed opposite, broke a biscuit on top of the porridge and spooned it.

The Cutter tells me you're an alright fella.

He looked up to see a pair of feet beside his head and then a face leaning down. The man stretched his toes and slinked his backside down from above and sat beside him on the bed.

I never said no such thing, The Cutter said. Stay away from him Snodgrass. Dangerous so he is.

The Cutter's laugh huge and hoarse. The man smiled and licked his lips with a flickering gray tongue then offered a hand that became a vigorous squeeze.

Aye. Call me Snodgrass, he said.

Alright then Snodgrass.

What's yer story then?

None such.

Where are ye for then?

Who knows.

Do you have people over there?

Naw. Yourself?

Oh no, The Cutter said.

What's that? said Coyle.

You'll start him off again.

Snodgrass smiled and his eyes glittered and his hand dipped into a pocket. It emerged clutching a yellowing envelope. I'm going to join my wee brother. He wrote to me so he did.

Snodgrass took the letter out of the envelope and handed it to Coyle. It was smudged with thumb prints and the folds of the paper were wearing through.

You can read it if you like.

Yer alright so you are.

The Cutter chimed in. Go on. It's your turn now. He canny read.

Coyle opened it and looked at it and saw Snodgrass beaming. Then he read out loud.

My Dear Bob. Come to swate Amerikay and come quickly. Here you can buy praties two shillings a bushel, whisky and coal same price, because we ain't got no turf here, a dollar a day for digging and no hanging for staling. Och now do come. Your dear brother James.

He didn't mention the price of the hoors, said The Cutter. I hope they're cheaper than here. There was a hoarse laugh and Snodgrass scowled and he took back the letter. Then he looked up. Hey boys, he said.

The Cutter answered him guttural. What.

Twelve days since we're gone.

What talent. The man can count.

The men snickered. Snodgrass looked down at the letter, held it with great delicacy, like it was something alive from nature or something that housed the living essence of a thing, and he folded it carefully with thick fingers and put it in his pocket. He looked at Coyle, excitement playing in his eyes.

Jamesy couldna read nor write hardly when he left but he must have been learning. Oh I canny wait. Do any of yous boys want to do a trade for tobacco?

A DAMP BLANKET OF DRIZZLE fell stippling the sea. The world a dour gray and he stood in line with The Cutter awaiting the fire to cook their food waving the bitter smoke out of their eyes. A storm of shouting erupted in front of them and The Cutter walked towards it—a dark-haired boy by the caboose stood slant-eyed and cursing his mother. The boy a head taller though he was not yet his full height and he had thrown his shoulders into the air like he had the cut of a man. His mother cringed and he threw a plate of food to the ground and then he lifted a hand in the air to strike her.

The Cutter stepped forward quick and he grabbed the boy's wrist from behind him and the boy snapped around and cursed him and he turned back around and swore at his mother and he shook himself free of the arrest. He hurled venomous glances at the eager eyes of the crowd and he turned and ran away. The spilt stew shining on the deck and the woman dropped her knees down into it and she began to plead with The Cutter. Please master do not punish him. He's wild so he is and there's just the two of us. He donny mean it.

Her voice was hollowed out, brittle like rotting wood. She bent her head and made the sound of weeping, though Coyle saw there were no tears in her eyes and The Cutter threw his hands into the air and he looked at the watching faces and walked away.

TIME DRAPED ITSELF languorously on top of them so that the world mercurial did its merry dance but the days passed the same. Four weeks the journey might take, or eight they were told, the nights beginning to numb and then one night no different than any other he was awoken from his sleep. The pitch dark animate with the drone of sleeping men and the sonorous sound of the sea. He sensed movement beside him furtive and his ears pricked, a soft scuffle rat-like and the noise abated and he waited and then it began again—a stealthy persistence he knew was no animal. His body tensed and he tried to sharpen his ears and in his mind he sensed the figure of a man between the cots. Silently he shifted his weight onto his side and then he kicked out his leg. There was a staccato yelp pitched high like a dog and in the fear that came upon him he went down upon it, found himself on top of a man grappling blindly in the dark. He found hold of an arm and locked it behind the man's back and he wrestled to get a hold of the other, took a sharp back kick to his shin and the breath went out of him. He loosened his grip and secured it again and he heard men start to awaken. The Cutter reached beneath him and found a box of lucifer matches and seized upon a match and lit it. It flamed brightly but was meager against the darkness and Snodgrass followed with the lighting of his own and in the dim light they saw the face of Coyle holding in restraint the arms of another. The man near face-down on the floor lying over the men's baggage.

The Cutter slid his legs from the top bed and landed upon the floor. He tossed the match and lit another and held the flickering flame faint towards the other's face. The Mute. Teeth and gums baring.

You, The Cutter said angrily. He let the match burn to his fingers and lit another.

Ye thieving fuck, he said and he went to hit him but he stopped himself. The Mute wriggled to be free and some of the men sat up on their beds while others called out for them to be quiet.

In the flickering match light Snodgrass sat up and began to light his pipe. Coyle stood The Mute up and The Cutter searched him and found nothing but the man's knife and he took it. Won't be needing this, he said. Where's that brother of yours?

Word went around and it came back that he was sleeping and Coyle let go of The Mute who slinked back into the thick wad of darkness.

Good man Inishowen, said The Cutter.

Just heard something that's all. I didn't know what he was up to.

Up to no good so he was the fucking thief. We'll have to keep an eye on him. Lock up your stuff boys.

Talk to the brother of his the morrow, said Coyle.

Either a talking or a drowning. I'll bloody do it myself.

The men went back to their beds and curled cramped, their minds wrestling with thoughts of sleep but their hearts beat as restless as the sea.

NOBLE GROWLED A WORD that sounded like cards and he produced and waved a pack and then he spat tobacco on the floor. The Cutter grumbled and swung stiffly off his cot and stood up with his back covered in straw. Snodgrass and Coyle leaned in and they lifted luggage to fashion a makeshift table and The Cutter began to dust himself. Noble started to cut the pack when Sam Tea leaned in beside them. The man carried more muscle than The Mute but he was the weaker brother of the two and he nodded to the men, his face all serious while Coyle nudged The Cutter.

Listen boys, he whispered. I'm sorry about that wee incident the other night.

They looked at his red-rimmed eyes all earnest and caught the whiskey on his breath.

What are ye whispering for? said The Cutter almost shouting.

Tea cringed and put his hand in the air as if to quieten the man and then he looked behind him.

We were wondering when you might say something, said Coyle. I'd begun to take odds from the men. If you'd come tomorrow I'd have made a few shillings.

Tea shrugged then scratched his nose. There's not much I canny do with him but I do my best with him.

Noble began to deal the cards and the men each picked up a hand and Tea nodded to the table.

What are yous playing? he asked.

Twenty-five.

Tea nodded. There was a wee bit of trouble back home so we had to go.

What was it he done? The Cutter asked. Can I take a wild guess?

Tea's head dropped and he spoke almost inaudible. He was caught thieving, he said.

The men said nothing. The Cutter looked at his cards and played a seven of spades and he made an animal squeal of excitement. He looked up smiling. That's a fucking surprise. Tell him to stay well away from here or I swear he's going to get it.

Coyle looked up at The Cutter but said nothing. Tea looked at the deck and then he nodded and his arm fished into his pocket and he produced a flask. I hear ye, he said. Wee sup?

HE LAY ON HIS COT troubled by memory. His father handling that horse old and forlorn on its feet. The mare dappled gray and its frame shrunken with age and the old man nursing it gently from the edge of the field with aim towards the stables. The horse walked stiff and slow until it stopped in the middle of the yard and he whispered to it encouragement but the horse was arthritic and its rheumy eyes spoke that it would go no further for now.

Coyle left his father's side and returned with straw in his hand and he offered it flat to the mouth of the animal but the horse showed no interest. The boy looked up at his father and the man looked back at the boy and he shook his head and spoke softly into the ear of the horse, pleaded to no avail, for the horse was like rock now resisting and the intransigence of the animal became too long for the man's liking and he pleaded further and less quietly and then what he dreaded most. From the big house the shutting of a door and then the shape of Faller and young Hamilton walking with his head cocked before him. The foreman's eyes fixed on the scene and as they neared the father cursed the beast and then spoke an apology to it and he pulled at it one more time but the horse looked at him sadly.

Young Hamilton just half a head taller. That's all he was. Bastard. Must have been no more than fourteen. The way he drew near that horse grinning, the long snout of Faller's gun dipping heavy in his hand. Coyle had looked at the gun, saw that it was barreled twice and he watched how the boy struggled with it and the towering man lean in to cock the weapon for him. Put it to the head, he said. The gunshot smacked the walls and jolted the boy who put his hands to his ears and when he turned around again he watched with ringing ears the mechanics of the horse cease to function, its knees crumple and its legs unspool from under it as the creature collapsed onto its side, one leg flickering briefly and then it became still but for its blood which was bright and glossy and pooling about their feet. Faller put the gun back in his belt and looked briefly at young Hamilton who stood proudly and then he turned to Coyle's father.

I told you about that old horse. Have somebody clean it up.

The pair of them walking back to the house together.

HE SLEPT AND WOKE from shallow sleep with the small fingers of his daughter in his hand. Her face liminal before him in that dark hold, the red rose of her lips and the sea rings of her eyes the very same as her mother and he could feel her body nimble with energy in his lap. He sat up awake. The bed cramped and his back ached and he scratched his face. The ship yawing deeper now than before. He lay back down and heard a whisper towards him. Inishowen? The Cutter's voice smiling in the dark. Are you awake?

Naw. Fast asleep so I am. What about ye? I thought ye were sleeping.

I went for a wee walk. Off getting myself seen to. Bit lighter now on me feet.

You and everybody else in here. The whole boat will tip over if all our money keeps going to those hoors in the women's quarters.

He heard The Cutter shifting his weight and then the man sidled down onto the bunk beside him. I've been thinking, The Cutter said.

What you been thinking?

The sooner we get off this boat the better.

Did you come up with that yourself?

Aye. Been pondering it all night.

You keep pondering then.

He heard The Cutter rustling about for his pipe.

Been pondering you too so I have.

No wonder you can't sleep.

Aye. Well. Wondering what kind of strange beast ye are because I canny figure.

That's great so it is.

I've known types to be on the run but you donny strike me as one of them.

Who says I'm on the run?

The Cutter shunted a compressed whisper in the dark towards Snodgrass. Hey boy. I know yer awake. Give me your matches.

His request was met by silence and The Cutter reached out and poked the sleeping man. There was a groan and a mutter and Snodgrass found his voice in the dark. What do ye want?

The Cutter reached out and ribbed the lying man again. Matches, he said.

Yer an awful cunt so ye are. Here, he said. A rattle in the dark and The Cutter grasped blindly and he found the hand and took them.

Anyways, he said.

The Cutter tamped down his pipe and struck a match but it went out again. Coyle sat up. The Cutter struck another and put it to his pipe. He sucked on it in the dark. Gimme here. Coyle took the pipe and toked on it.

I hope it was worth it, The Cutter said.

What was?

Whatever it was that you did.

Why's that?

Because once you get to where we're going you're hardly likely to get back.

That's great so it is. I ask you to buy me a ticket and you have to go and get one for the boat that is going away the furthest. Real considerate.

There was no other passenger boat sailing. Anyhow, I needed the company. Here have a wee toke on this now and shut up.

THE DAYS BLURRED INDISTINCT from one another. And then the rain, the relentless sound of it. He imagined mountains of small stone being loosed ceaselessly upon the deck, loosed steady for two days now. It made cooking on the deck impossible, produced a restlessness that pressed down upon them in their hunger, filled the air and gnawed at them until it left them more enfeebled than before. They ate raw what they could and heard word of men from the family quarters swearing trouble if they could not feed properly their wives and children. A man stout and elderly led a delegation to the ship's master who met the minor insurrection with the proud jut of his jaw. He made an order for more grog to be released and then he turned his back and the men took to drunkenness and cursed the sea and the weather and they cursed their hunger. They drank too the water that had become foul, corrupting in wine casks until it sat in their cups like thin tea, muddied and bitter, and after a time some of them stopped drinking it. The Cutter threw his cup of water across the room and some of the men cheered. Gimme some matches, he said.

They heard a report from Snodgrass that a man had the fever. And then talk of a woman. Word traveled on worried faces and then there were two more among their own in the hold. At night Coyle listened, the wind wrapping a sough around the keening timbers of the ship and the grim sound of the stricken. The sawtoothed groan of a man for want of water throughout the night and the mumbles of another incomprehensible. Their voices like wraiths in the darkness, circling unseen but felt above the rest of them dozing fitful or wide-eyed in their beds and in the morning his mind would race to breathe in the calm report of the sea.

HE STOOD ON DECK in the mesh of his thoughts, his eyes fixed numbly on the sea, the impossibility of what it presented. The image of Hamilton falling against stone. The child by the door crying. And what he saw of his brother Jim. I shouldn't have listened to Ranty. Should have gone back home. Should have lived my life quietly. Shoulda just gone and left. But maybe Ranty was right. I am still alive and I can send for them. And maybe she will forgive me for what I have done though I did not plan any of it. And deep in his being he fought against a deeper drift of thought, something phantom and unseen that traveled through him darkly, the surety that Faller would come after him.

And he thought of his father sinking into the water, the calm indifference of the river surrounding, the face of his father plunging into the smooth gray flanks, the eyes he remembers rigid with terror as they came back to the surface momentarily, his hands reaching for something, the liquid that would not give hold, the horse calmly swimming. The boy who just stood there watching, aware of the other man who had come at a sprint down the bank, who stood there shouting that he didn't know how to swim, and the boy grappling with the enormity of the moment, his impotency in the face of it, cannot remember if he was able even to shout, and the realization that his father would not be coming

back up. And him just standing there not doing anything.

The Cutter poked him in the ribs. Yer away off someplace.

Just thinking.

THE CUTTER CUT CARDS and shuffled and dealt to the
two others three cards at a time followed by two. The
cards in the pack he stacked face down on the valise
and he turned the top card face up. Two of spades.
Spades are trumps boys. The men leaned over to pick
up their cards. Snodgrass sat down beside them on the
bed and leaned in and whispered. Sounds like the older
Tea brother has got the fever, he said. He rubbed his jaw
with the back of his hand and looked at the other men.
Smudged cards pressed together between forefinger and
thumb, eyes watching intently. Coyle played the two of
diamonds and in the same breath the diamond queen.
He looked up. For sure?

Aye.

Noble sat quiet chewing on tobacco and kept his
cards close to his face. He fingered the queen of spades
and played it and then worked his mouth and spat tobacco onto the floor. He whispered loudly. The Mute
spent the night sitting at Sam's bed. I saw meself when I
got up for a piss.

The Cutter placed a three of spades and smiled.
Could be just visiting. For a chat, like.

He's a great talker alright, said Coyle. The men giggled. The Cutter put down a two of clubs. An awful
one for the idle chatter, he said. Snodgrass looked back
over his shoulder. There was a lot of moaning coming
from Sam during the night, he said. It wasna night-
mares.

Got it bad do you think?

Bad enough by the sounds of it.

When they were finished playing Coyle walked over
to the cot to see. The Mute just sitting there backturned
and Coyle stole behind him all quiet. He saw Sam Tea,
his feet and ankles swollen out of all natural proportion
and his face and hands peppered with dark spots pur-
plish in the faint light. His lips were parched and his
mouth worked feverish whispers for water and Coyle
walked on and when he returned he threw a glance casual and found The Mute staring.

THE FIRST MATE WENT among them with water and the
men cursed him under their breaths for the filthy piss
it was but they drank it anyway. He returned in the
afternoon, master's grog he said, and he went around
collecting money from their outstretched dirty hands.
They held their cups out and slugged thirstily on the
watered-down brew and the men watched the mate with
mean eyes but they said nothing. Coyle stood up and
told him there was another man sick and he pointed to
the cot and the first mate nodded. What's his name? he

said. The first mate put down the pitcher and took out a black notebook from his shirt pocket and penciled a note.

THE SEA MORE RESTLESS than before and they sensed the weather turning. The men huddled to make merry, the hold draped in candlelight and the smoke ghosting above their heads and they scratched at the lice in their hair and dug their nails into the bedbugs that sucked on them through their clothes. They slurped messily on their cups, the contents pitching and splashing contrary to the leanings of the ship, their beards wet with grog, and they clamored voluminously over each other's voices, each one wanting to be heard, the hearing of one's voice a kind of fortitude to drown out all other noises—the groans of the sick, the intimations of invisible violence in the wind, their own silence that whispered of their powerlessness.

He watched two friends begin to wrestle on the floor and when it turned to blows the men were pulled off one another. The others told stories. A group of them huddled in a loose circle by the cots and he sat down among them and listened. Two brothers identical and one of them called Joe and the other John and both of them with the kind of glint in the eye that relished confusion. Joe was telling a story from home and John kept interrupting.

It went on for months so it did, said Joe. You'd be dying to tell her but you couldna. It was part of the fun of it. You'd go across that moss at Whitetown and you'd find her house in a parting of trees. The old boy long dead.

She had no idea, said John. A year it went maybe. You'd be hoping for a moon. Otherwise you'd hardly know where you'd be going.

Knock three times on the door.

Aye that was it. That was the code.

The men laughed. The Cutter sat down and took out his pipe. Snodgrass passed him a box of matches.

She was wild stupid so she was. She'd do anything you'd tell her, said Joe.

John shook his head at the memory of her. Silly bitch, he said. Just a wee whimper of complaint out of her and that was all.

Bring an animal into the room and she woulda.

You did not did you?

Naw. I'm just sayin.

She must have been mad for it, said Snodgrass.

Let's just say she was wild compliant, said Joe. Do you remember the way she smelt? Her hair smelt like new grass. Skin smelling like the way it does after it stops raining.

We used to swap nights so we did, said John.

We did it first as a wee notion, just for the joke of it because John was seeing her first and told me about her. To see would she notice, the silly bitch. But then we kept it up. Always in the dark though. For fear she'd figure us out. She'd moan out oh John, oh John, and of course I was Joe.

What are ye on about? There was only ever a wee whimper out of her.

She'd say oh John you're much bigger tonight. And I'd be tempted to tell her I was Joe.

The men shook with laughter and John drove a big fist into the leg of his brother. Behind them they heard Sam Tea groan for water.

And then there was the time we were both away, said Joe. I was up working a farm in Dunfanaghy. And John was working away for the day in Miltown. I had the horn wild bad. It was a bright night all lit up by the moon.

Naw, there wasn't. It was dark so it was.

So what. I remember weighing it up but in the end I walked the extra few miles. Me feet aching under me. I got to the door and knocked three times. She was slow to open and I was beginning to wonder if she had gone away. And then the door pulled back slowly and the re-action out of her. I stood there with a wee grin on me face and told her I'm bursting for ya and she put a hand to her mouth and next thing she was off, not a sound out of her, mind, just off out into the night, running and nothing but a shawl on her past me out into the darkness.

John spoke. I was lying on the bed with her and next thing you know there are three knocks on the door.

The men laughed, wheezing like a pack of dogs.

We never went back to her after that. She probably died in the cold of fright.

Behind them Sam Tea groaned. Coyle turned around and saw The Mute glowering at the men. He stood up and walked over stepping roughly on the men's belongings and he slapped Snodgrass's cup out of his hand. The contents splashed onto the heads of the men and the cup crashed off the floor and the men roared indignantly. Snodgrass stood to his feet as if to fight. Coyle stood up and put a hand on the man's shoulder, his voice firm but quiet. Leave it.

Snodgrass shook his shoulder. I will not.

Sit down, he said. And you, he said pointing to The Mute. Sit yourself back down there and quit causing trouble. You make a lot of noise for a man who canny talk.

The Mute just stared at him and then he walked closer. Coyle felt the man's breath on his face and he spoke to him again. Go and sit yourself down and quit this nonsense.

Some of the men giggled and Noble stood up and pulled The Mute by the arm until he was led away.

Joe shook his head. Och to be back in that bed with that silly bitch. John smiled but his eyes began to glaze and inwardly he traveled the thousands of miles home and as he did his smile fell silently from his face.

THE WORLD THAT WAS ALL SKY was leaded and sinking fast and the sun was nowhere to be seen. Around noon came the sound that many dreaded, the snapping shut of the hatches and the ventilators to keep watertight the boat, the scuffle of tarpaulin on the deck and the dull thud of pitched weights. Nothing to suck on now but the air tombed beneath.

The master watched the sky swirl and he bellowed commands in a broad voice that was torn up and scattered by the wind. The ship scudded headlong into the squall. Mountains rose out of the sea, reached up towards the sky as if it wanted to take the smudged remnants of the heavens into its quickening mouth, a sea of jagged teeth.

The waters became then what was the world, invisible hands tormenting it, a dark-slated churning that sucked the ship down deep and spat it out again. The Murmod heeled and its beams bent groaning with the exertion and almost every man but the master feared that it would break apart. The sailors fought with a strength supernatural as if they had become incubi feeding on the strength of all those below who could do nothing but remain in their bunks, nausea and mind sickness pitching each single one of them in that darkness with dead weight down into his own inert void. They lay with fear drowning their spirits, some of them bent double, vomiting into what buckets there were or upon themselves and their bedding. Some tried to light candles but the oakum wicks would not stay lit, were tossed about in their saucers of fat, and children cried and women wept and men shushed them but they too were afraid and in the men's quarters they wanted to reach out to each other for comfort but did nothing.

A woman found her way to the door of the hold, held on to it, a flickering candle in her hand and her voice shy. She called to the man nearest her and he took the name and passed it on till a man got up from a bunk and went towards her.

I know that man, Snodgrass said. That's his sister he's going to.

Day became a night of pounding darkness. The wind burled around the boat, a coven of riled witches said one woman, the rain venomous and cat-spitting upon the deck. The men in their thirst and hunger produced what alcohol they had left and they shared their cups with one another and tried to drink away their anxiety. The sound of their voices rose in unison as their blood was sluiced with drink, a solidarity of shouting to quell the noise of the storm, but their spirits foundered as the night wore on, their voices lowering till there was just the occasional talk as the men lay wide-eyed for lack of sleep, lay listening to the howling sky.

I don't want to die, said Snodgrass.

You're not going to die, said Coyle.

How'd you know it?

I just know it so I do.

The ship pitched and shuddered and the men were silent and then Snodgrass's voice in the smothering darkness. Kilt in the middle of the sea where nobody will know that I'm gone and I won't get no burial.

No sleep at all and then night became day, no reprieve and the trapped air around them thinning to be filled by the thickening fetor of their own dirt, a reeking butyric stench all sweat and stale urine while excrement slopped in brimmed buckets. Little food to be had and what they had left could not be kept down and they clung to their cots, some of the men grim and silent and others wailing an animal-like sound weak against the fury outside, and Coyle lay there curling into his own body as if he could protect himself from the elements, began to think of the firs. The size of them as he walked that time on his own after seeing his father drown, carrying with him the last look of his father's eyes, and how he slept in the hollow of a fallen oak tree, pulled the leaves into a damp blanket around his body and fought against his memory. And that day Coyle remained sleepless though the world a dream until he noticed that despite his nausea the roaring wind was only a whisper and the rain had softened into a hiss that became silent and he thought of that morning when he awoke no longer a boy and he climbed out of that ragged carcass of a tree.

They emerged red-eyed and silent into the rinsed evening air, their clothes ragged and their bodies bent and their faces creased with dirt. They stared with disbelief at the great waters silent, smoothed with a benevolent repose, and they looked with distrust towards the sun that glittered warmly in the pale blue sky, moved awkward through its gift of pure air. Women huddled and began to find their voices and some of the men took off their shirts and they sat bare-chested on the deck goose-fleshed by the breeze while another lay down with his arms outstretched like he was a man awaiting crucifixion. The cabooses were lit and a rough queue formed of quarrelsome people, the clang and scrape of pot and pan and the hacking sounds of coughing.

COYLE LISTENED TO THE GROANS of the sick reach from below and he thumbed the ribbon in his hand. He stood with a handful of others watching the sail master at work, the old man pocked and lobster-faced and he bent to work with nimble fingers about the bodies that had been taken up from below—a woman and a boy, each claimed by fever and their faces swelled up like they were full of the sea. The sail master took no notice of the crowd's watching, scuttled sideways like a crab about the bodies and licked the tips of his fingers as he worked, mummifying both in white sail, and he called in scuffed voice to another sailor to tie weights about their ankles. The mother of the child was watching dead-eyed the sail-wrapping of the body, her body stiff and her shawl in her hands and her hair blowing in her face. Behind her the child's father stood haggard and white-knuckled and when the sail master worked the last stitch of the shroud, a needle to pierce through the rubbery flanks of nostril and seal the body of air, he shuddered with a groan and fell into the arms of another.

Coyle watched the young man who had quit his bed

during the night to aid his sister stand now over her sail-coffined body. His lips trembling and he kept his arms folded as the wind pronged his hair and then he dropped to his knees and went to her softly and brought the shrouded corpse up to him.

A crowd assembled and the master of the ship emerged with one arm in his jacket and he sleeved the loose limb and buttoned the garment and he checked that the bodies were ready for ceremony. His face was crumpled and red-eyed from tiredness and his white hair glistened uncombed in the hard noon sun. His face was freshly shaven and he pinched the smooth flesh on his jaw and he coughed to get attention. A small black bible and he hurried a few words and then he closed the book with the words still in his mouth and he turned and nodded to four sailors in peacoats behind him. They bent to the bodies and took the shrouded woman first, counted to three and lifted the remains onto a pair of nailed planks. They carried the remains at shoulder height to the bulwark and hoisted her aslant amidst hush. They did not need to count for the lifting of the child, the body featherlight upon the boards, and they hoisted it too up over the side of the deck, the faceless remains sliding off the wood and fluttering softly as if caressed by the breeze, before the thin lips of the ocean parted to take the child down into the deep.

HE WAS SNOOZING noontime in his bunk when he felt a hand on his shoulder. Snodgrass leaning over him eyes broad with excitement and The Cutter climbing down from the bunk above. Noble leaned over the side of the bed and spat tobacco. What's the fuss? he said. The Cutter shouted, Quit that spitting would ya. Snodgrass pointed upwards. Come see.

They saw the fin in the ocean when it was pointed out to them. A dark glistening gray, a steady ripple along the surface of the water and foam gentle in its wake. The men spoke of the shark in whispers as if the creature could hear the words they were saying.

It's following us a day now, said Snodgrass. Don't tell no one.

The men looked at him. Coyle leaned his head in and smiled. We'll get the ship's master to announce it.

Snodgrass winced. That's not funny. That thing can't be up to no good.

The men watched the line of the shark, constant, deliberate, as the ship tacked under gray sky. They sat and played cards and they ate and when they were done they gathered again to see. At seven o'clock the first mate poured water upon the deck fires, steam hissing up into the riled faces of those with dinners half cooked, and they grumbled and took their ware and vittles below. The men beckoned to the mate and he walked over and they pointed to the shark.

Aye, he sighed. I seen that already.

The Cutter looked to the mate. Hey how about this?

He tapped Snodgrass on the shoulder. How long is it?
Forty-nine days.

The Cutter pointed at Snodgrass's head. Impressive isn't he? Regular as a clock.

Snodgrass scrunched his nose baring yellowing ridged teeth and he squeezed his ears like he was trying to squeeze out the sound of The Cutter. He turned to the mate. What's it up to? he said. The creature.

The first mate picked his nose and rolled his findings between finger and thumb and flicked it upon the wind. He looked at the shark fin cutting darkly the water and he shrugged and took a sniff of the air. His blue eyes full of knowing.

I'd say that thing following us is a sure sign of death.

EVENING KISSED THE burning darkness. From dim inferno of western sky sprawled a reaching fog. He watched it take hold and settle upon them, a phantom pall that turned night sky to dust and muffled the sea to silence. He lay deadened throughout the night, his body awkward turning, his mind slumbered with shallow and shapeless dreams, and he would awake, his breath frosted in the foul air and he would wrap his arms about himself from the cold and listen to the terrors of the night. The desolate lament of the ship's foghorn sounding across a hushed sea and the ceaseless chorus of the sick, solo voices rising rabid and raving above stifled groans, the clamors of the delirious and the dying rising out from their berths to nestle amidst the ghosted sea. And then the tolling of the ship's bell, grim-sounding as if they had come to a place that was not godless ocean at all but graveyard consecrated and the ship groaning had become a lurching vessel for the dead.

In the morning he heard that Sam Tea had died during the night. They said the man was discovered with his eyes and mouth open as if he was in shock at his own passing. Swelling had so disfigured the man that no person would help in the removal. The Mute had disappeared from his post by the invalid's bed and the body lay uncovered till the first mate came down to the hold. They found The Mute hunched over his heels in a corner at the other end of the ship, his face scrunched mean and his fists balled on his knees. He would acknowledge the presence of no other, not even the first mate, who made to arrange his brother's burial and who called upon an older man who bunked beside the bereaved to console him. The man put a hand onto his shoulder but The Mute twitched and turned and spat violently upon the ground.

HIGH CLOUDS DUSTED a distant sky so that it seemed they were sailing aslant some great snow-laden mountain. The sail master went to work spit-fingered on Sam Tea and the bodies of two others, was heard to complain from his hollow red cheeks that he was running out of sail. When he was finished they gathered on deck and the master appeared and they waited for The Mute but he was not to be found and the first mate and another went looking for him. They returned without him, said he was not going to be coming, and the master shrugged and committed the bodies to the sea, indifference on his face and hunger written on the faces of all the others.

HE SAT ON THE DECK with his legs crossed beneath him and he chewed on griddle-cake. The surface burnt black and the centre raw and he champed through it and worked the clots over with his tongue while watching. Mothers putting patties of food into the small hands of children who took the offerings and ate quietly. Beneath their matted hair and the filth on their moppet faces he could make out their pallid skin, their eyes shored like small stones by gray pools, not children now in the way they behaved but like the elderly—light of bone but their bodies weighted invisible with lethargy. Across from him a woman sat with an infant on her breast. The child's feet were woolen-booted and a small boy with skyward hair leaned his swollen eyes upon his mother's shoulder. A shaft of light cut by the mast fell and made tender the side of her face and he watched her eat and feed the boy porridge, both of them feeding from the flat of her hand, the woman not seeing his gaze at all but looking beyond him to the kiss of the sea and sky, the skin of an older woman rutted and grooved on a young woman's face. She started coughing and then she saw him looking and smiled.

Do you have any of yer own? she said.

Aye. A wee girl. Coyle held his hand a distance above the deck as if to demonstrate the child's height.

Did you leave her behind?

Had to.

The woman nodded. You can send for her surely when you get settled. I heard there's lots who do that.

As she spoke the softness fell from his face. Mark you me, Coyle said. She's not going to grow up not knowing who I am. I swear that to you now on me grave.

HE SAT IN HIS BARE FEET picking the dirt in his fingernails, Snodgrass silent beside him and their backs upon the bulwark. The deck was quieter than usual, the sea worked by a tender breeze and the bow of the ship nodding in agreement. And then The Cutter was upon them and heavyboned he dropped down sending both men toppling. Snodgrass cursed him and Coyle knuckled him in the leg and The Cutter laughed. Food on his plate and he began to eat with his hands. Coyle looked at him. Ya dirty-fingered bastard ya.

The Cutter finished his food and set the plate down beside him and then he nudged Coyle softly with his elbow. Over yonder, he said.

What is it?

Donny turn your head.

I think I know.

The Mute.

Aye.

But I'll knock the fucking eyes out of his head.

Might make him talk.

But then again it mightn't.

Coyle worked his nails again, pretended not to see. I just want to keep the peace, he said. He's been at that now this past few days.

Snodgrass looked over at The Mute.

Would ye stop looking at him, Coyle said.

I'm gathering from the way he's looking at you he doesn't like you, said Snodgrass.

That's a prize mind you got in that head of yours, said Coyle.

Go an fuck, said Snodgrass.

The Cutter rubbed his nose with the back of his hand. He can't still be sore about that time, he said.

Back to his old ways again, said Coyle.

Like a bad dog.

Why would he wait till now?

There might be more to it than you figure.

I've had no other dealings with him.

Who knows what's going on in that mind of his? It's not as if he's going to tell anyone about it.

Maybe someone can ask him to draw it.

He AWOKE NEAR MIDNIGHT and noticed the rain at peace and he stood up and shook The Cutter and they went up to the deck for air. A small crowd already gathered and the two men speechless at what they saw. It was not the world anymore but the world upended. Sky where sea should be and the waters alive as if the stars had plummeted from their fixings and left the night canvas an empty black. The ocean glowed molten-white like liquid fire unquenchable. The phosphorescence spread out around them in fields of phantom light, each rippling wave crested with a line of the same peculiar sight that shot up the prow of the ship as the bow sliced the water, a leaping luminescence as if the sea had become a living thing stretching lustrous and tingling that fizzled out on the night air.

From the masts and rigging fell shadows sinister and the boat a whisper on the water. Hushed too were the onlookers, twenty or so, with puzzled brows and eyes wide in wonder. The master stood on the deck alongside his wife and she whispered to those near her in a voice of calm authority that she'd seen this wonder of the sea before but never quite this remarkable and isn't it the most wondrous thing and nearby The Cutter spoke, his voice quiet and respectful.

I donny know whether to be terrified or in awe of it.

A man beside them whispered. The sailors are saying

it is a natural sight of the warmer waters. They say it means that we're near Amerikay.

Coyle whispered. There's more mysteries to this world than I'd have ever thought.

The Cutter whispered back. And do you know what?

What?

The fish aren't getting a wink of sleep.

They stood and watched till the east blotched blue and flared and when they went down into the hold and lay restless in their beds, their minds stretching to accommodate this sight that filled them with fear and wonder, they thought of those left behind at home and the stories they would like to tell and how they would put the sight of it into words. And when finally he fell to sleep that night, Coyle dreamed of the sea, the waters white-hot and burning brightly about his body, and then the dream darkened until they were sailing through waters that became the deepest dye of red.

HE WATCHED THE white tips of the water chesting forward, a thing of foaming beauty alive for one brief moment and then they turned in on themselves, the ceaseless renewal of the sea. Behind him a woman came upon the deck, toothless she was and her head was shorn and he turned and then he watched her. She ferried clothes folded over her arm to a spot where she began to lay them out, each item one by one on the boards, and then she stood up and called out and began to auction them. Each item was lifted and held and examined. A woman hardly taller than a child held the white dress up to her body, the sleeves drooped past her hands and the hem of the dress bundled about the deck. She negotiated a price and drew a string-tied purse from around her neck and put the money into the woman's outstretched hand. Other items disappeared until there was a black shawl left. He watched a young mother produce a coin and take the garment. She walked over to the other side of the deck and wrapped it tenderly about the shoulders of a coughing child.

The short woman appeared on deck wearing her new dress, the material dragging behind her, and two boys began to follow standing on the flowing hem until it rose up as she walked and trapped her. The men laughed at the sight until Snodgrass wagged a finger. Don't be laughing at her, he said. She's wearing a dead woman's dress.

They sat and watched evening lay itself out against the sky, the far reaches of the empty world lit up by the silent burning sun. The snow-dusted clouds grew dark so that it looked like it would rain. By the caboose, a child rummaged about the leavens. The air grew cold and they went down to the hold where they lay on their bunks.

The Cutter called over to the bunk opposite.

Snodgrass.

What.

Will you tell me how long is it?

Naw.

Please I want to know.

Snodgrass held off for a moment and then he spoke. Sixty-one days.

The Cutter lit his pipe and smoked it and then passed it to Coyle and he toked on it and passed it back. They lay down on their backs wishing silently for the journey to pass.

HE AWOKE, HIS MIND alert and he found he couldn't sleep. Most of the men were slumbered and a stillness about so that it seemed the sick and the dying had agreed upon a temporary kind of peace. He climbed out over the luggage sprawl and stepped quietly onto deck, the air silken and virtuous and it nestled against him. His nostrils widened and he breathed it in deeply. The dark clouds had rolled back to reveal the starry canvas, a jeweled rug that glittered with the selfsame stars he looked upon as a child, and he leaned upon the bulwark and gazed upon it.

Footsteps and a figure came towards him in the darkness. He saw it was a man and he put his hand into the air in welcome and he received no signal in return. No way of determining who it was in the dim light until the man was nearly on top of him and he saw then it was The Mute. A shiv in his hand and he cut the air in front of him with a swipe and then he lunged silently at Coyle. Skim of knife on flesh and searing ribs and Coyle back-pedaled away from him. The Mute lunged again and

Coyle made a grab for the outstretched arm, caught it and the two men locked. Their muscles flexed and their arms shuddered, for a moment each man seeming not to breathe. And they wrestled wordless but for the exertion that rose out of each man guttural, their necks goitered and their nostrils snorting and the only other sound was the plashing of waves.

He rose a knee up into the groin of his attacker and he felt the man weaken and he squeezed the arm and bent it and the shiv fell to the deck and he looked his assailant in the eye but in the darkness there was nothing to see.

There was a thud and the two men fell backwards and Coyle lost his balance and went to the ground and when he looked up he saw the shape of another, The Mute taken by the throat and dragged abaft till the youngster was pitched over the edge of the ship. Coyle caught his breath and stood himself up with his hands on his knees panting. The Cutter. The Mute's feet off the ground and the air in his throat sealed by The Cutter's grasp.

Leave him, Coyle shouted.

The Cutter said nothing and grabbed a hold of The Mute by the belt with his other hand and yanked him up further over the edge. Coyle grabbed at the arm of The Cutter.

Donny I said.

This fucker.

It's not worth seeing him kilt.

I've seen enough.

Leave him.

I said I've seen enough of him.

Terror in The Mute's eyes and Coyle pulled again at the arm of The Cutter, his limbs hard as the bole of a tree, and then he let The Mute slide back to his feet. A sailor appeared and looked at The Mute on his hands and knees like a wheezing mutt and he stared at the two men and Coyle shrugged and walked away following the steps of The Cutter who had stormed ahead cursing darkly under his breath.

HE WATCHED THE LONELY sky give birth to life, a mote of dust that grew before his eyes into a fluttering living thing, a lone gull winging down from high. Black-tipped wing beat the air, bestrode the boat in glide and then it turned and plunged towards the sea. A day passed and more gulls came, swooped down to settle on the Murmod's masts and from the deck they watched the birds and then forgot about them. The birds settled and squawked and swung off again into the serene vastness beating their wings as if they were beating themselves free of life and he watched them till they had become nothing again.

Another day he sighted a vessel through squinted eyes flashing under the sun and the same evening he saw a flotilla of fishing sloops, short sails like fins cutting the water.

The sharks were gone but the ship had more dead to give. The first mate sent below a young sailor to count the fevered, for he himself would no longer go among them, and the sailor emerged with shaken green eyes and he gave his report with a tremor in his voice and he went to the side of the ship and was sick. The mate went and spoke to the sail master. The old man shrugged amidst rub of rustbeard and said he was out of sail. A corpse was carried up from below, the body of a woman whose face in death was ballooned and grotesque, her limbs bloated, and about her body hovered her son. They saw he was the same black-haired boy from before who swung his fist at her and he stood now with his arm by his side slobbering red-faced like a child. He begged her for forgiveness and he asked her for her blessing and then he turned upon the women who had swooped upon the body to pick it free of its clothes. A woman wrestled a shoe off a foot and made off with the other while another tugged at the dead woman's dress and the boy kicked at them until they stopped. They backed away and they called him a villain and a blackguard and a beater and told him he got what he deserved and the boy stared at them in gimlet-eyed fury, stood vigilant as her body was sheathed in sackcloth by the sail master and when her body was committed he stood uncomforted and howling.

THE MUTE FELT their gaze all the time, went nowhere now for everywhere the eyes watching. Saw them staring at him as he squatted over the bucket, knew they were watching him while he tried to sleep. He stayed put by his bed, did not visit the deck nor bother with daylight or the cooking of his food though nobody ever saw him eating anything at all cold or otherwise though some said they saw him drink. He sat on his cot with his knees under his chin or he lay on his back and they watched him go through again his brother's things. A mottled brown suitcase with squeaking clasps housed the dead man's clothing, a suit and trousers, a shirt, a hat, a pair of boots with the soles laughing and other items he spread out on the bed. He laid out an old newspaper and he held his brother's clay pipe in his mouth without lighting it and fixed his hair with a comb.

COYLE SAT PLAYING twenty-five with the others. Snodgrass cutting and dealing while sucking on his teeth and The Cutter distracted, eyeing up the cot of The Mute. Snodgrass turned over the top card. Hearts for trumps boys. Noble coughed and they picked up the cards silent and narrowed their eyes and played with quick fingers. The ship creaked and Snodgrass yelped. Twenty-five, he said. Coyle took the cards and cut them again and dealt.

The Cutter picked up his hand. You know what I'm thinking?

Coyle spoke without looking up from his cards. I know what you're thinking. You're figuring him for a man but he's still just a boy.

Aye. A boy who tried to kill ye.

That kid's wild so he is, said Noble. Like one of them horses gallivanting about that's got it funny in the head.

They whipped the cards around quick. Snodgrass played the jack of diamonds and beamed. That's me won again boys.

Coyle leaned back. He only grazed me that's all. And he ain't going to be doing nothing now anyhow.

I'll bet.

Lay off him will ye. We're nearly got to America and he already got what was coming to him, said Coyle.

No he ain't, said The Cutter.

You know what I mean.

The Cutter put down his cards and scrunched his fists. Noble you donny quit spittin that tobacco near my head and I'm going to mash it into your face.

A FAINT SHIMMERING SEEN through squinting eyes. The western rim of the world sprinkled with dust.

Land. Huppidy hah.

His breath grew heavy and he stood there for hours watching the new world rise imperceptibly out of the sea, a density solid forming, the ocean behind an infinity breached. He paid no heed to the people who gathered around him, and the many that came from below to watch, convalescents who were carried and put ragged standing onto the deck and leaning onto others for support. They sucked on the warm wind and stood in their awkwardness with their skin ashen and their eyes like pinholes while others began to sing and pray.

The ship nosed up the estuary, sailed past an island that humped out of the gulf white-flecked with gannets and gulls on the ridges of its back. The land a vague gray and closing slowly around them and the ocean a tapering stretch of blue behind. Low cloud pillowed with rain and it rolled in over the coast towards them and then they went below, the downpour thickening throughout the night and it washed the decks but failed to wash away their excitement.

SNODGRASS LEANED OVER the men, chewing on the corner of his lip. The Mute's gone, he said. The men leaned towards him. Noble puckered his lips and spat a wadge of tobacco onto the ground and he rolled up his sleeves. Gone where? he said.

Gone, said Snodgrass. Proper gone. No one's seen him about.

They went over to look, the cot empty and his belongings on the floor, and others stood about talking. Coyle looked at The Cutter and the man shrugged and they asked the old man who slept nearby. Spit on his lips when he spoke. I ain't seen him since I woke this morning. No sign of him. No sign of him at all. And no one's seen him anywhere.

I'm putting me name on the brother's suit if he donny come back, a man said behind them.

The first mate was sent for and another sailor came down, his face freckled and his jaw faintly whiskered, and he said the mate was busy and what is it that you want? The men told him about The Mute and the sailor looked at the bed and he shrugged and he turned and went away. The first mate came down and he grimaced at the smell and he looked at the bed and asked who had last seen him. No one could remember. He took out his notebook and wrote something down and then he went upstairs. He took two sailors and they began a search but found no sign of him and they decided he was lost.

The hold bustled with every kind of theory. The death of his brother is what done it for him, said one. Sure he was as good as dead anyhow, said another. What with him being mute, what kind of life is there for a man like that in Amerikay?

The twins fought with another man over the suitcase of clothes and Noble went over to the bunk and intervened. These'll all be auctioned, he said, and he took the items off the men and put them on the bed and then he began the sale. The men elbowed each way to get to the front and the bidding began and Coyle saw one of the brothers walk away with the boots laced about his neck.

He went to his bed and found The Cutter on it smoking his pipe.

Tell me what you know.

What do I know about what?

The Mute. The mystery of. Speak.

I reckon there's no mystery to it.

Do you reckon he leaped? said Snodgrass.

I reckon this man here knows otherwise, said Coyle.

The Cutter gave him a deep, hard look. Keep your reckoning to yourself for I had fuck all to do with it. I'd a been sorely tempted to do him in but I'm not that kind of man. He's likely gone and repented and he did it on his own. Or someone else could have done the repenting for him. That I wouldna be surprised about. But I had nothing to do with it.

Coyle stared at The Cutter and The Cutter hard-stared him back. Fuck you, he said. Snodgrass looked at both men and then clapped his hands. How about a game of cards boys?

Part III

I NEVER KNOWED ANYBODY THAT HAD EYES LIKE HIM. *The darkest shade of blue like just before night fallin. Sometimes I wake after seein him and I lie there tryin to hold on to the memory of his face. The only time I can see him clearly now is when I'm dreamin. Some nights it feels like I'm awake and I can see him sittin by the fire, his back to me, and I'd be talkin away to him but he never turns around and no matter how I look I canny see his face. And then you'd wake up and that terrible feelin would rush over you—the realization that he's gone and that another night has passed in an empty bed and that he might not never come back and I know I'll spend the whole day watching the fields.*

The newborn is the spit of him so he is but you canny know when he gets older what way his face is going to go. I see flashes of him sometimes, a glance in the eye, an expression, and then he's gone and other times he's right in front of me, right in front of me so he is, and I pull the child close to me and hug the life out of him.

I'll feel bad about what happened to my dying day so I will, for I could have done more to stop him. It were my fault he went away that time because I didn't get up and stop him. And that mother of his was only too keen for trouble but then she was wild bitter so she was.

I knew in my bones Coll did something wrong that day but I never believed that he kilt him. You see I knew what Coll was like, the way he had a temper on him. It would rise up out of him like a burst of bad weather and he'd go black for hours and then he'd come out of it. But he was never violent. And I never minded it because there was a big softness to him that he couldna hide. He was wild soft for the child. Others would not be like that at all. His brother, god rest him, would nearly kick his way through the weans just to get past them, and him so friendly and all with the horses. But Coll would soon as see a child and want to play with them. I remember one time him runnin around the field with the child on his shoulders, bouncing her about and swinging her up into the air. And he had this wee trick with his finger to make it disappear and she'd be left in a fit of giggles. Anyhow, where am I now? I need to tell you about a wee woman called Bridie Butler.

THE MAN CALLED HIMSELF Duffy and loomed large in front of them, his legs parted and hands on hips intimating with a smiling nod of his head he would not let any of them pass. His eyes glowed dark and a cigar sat fat and fuming on his heavy lips. Men of Erin, he said.

Come with me if you want to find work and I will make you your fortune.

They saw he was dressed in a suit knotted at the neck and wore a hat glossy and black. Listen up. The name's Duffy and I'm an Ulsterman like yourselves done good so I am and I can tell you now you will have a hard time doing good on your own without the likes of me so listen.

His voice boomed over the bustle and clatter of the quays and the men gathered around with nervous glances. Coyle nodded to The Cutter and they stood and listened to what the man had to say, saw behind him the city serene, a long line of storied buildings facing across the waterway. Church spires poked the sky and they looked at the competition of signs, Crooks Sperm and Polar Oil, Kending Willard & Co. Auctioneers, Neafie & Company of Philadelphia, and they saw Snodgrass being met by his brother, the man looking the spit of him and the two of them hugging for a minute and then Snodgrass waved farewell.

Come with me and I will give you work, Duffy said. Some of you don't know a soul here but now you know me. I will pay fifteen dollars a month to a man. That's real American money. The days are hard but the hours are fair and you will have fine canvas tents to sleep in. Fifteen dollars is plenty to be living on I can assure you. You will work for me six days of the week and you will have the Sabbath to yourselves. Plenty of food and all the whiskey you can buy and sure what more could a man want? All you'll be needing to bring are strong arms. Fit strong Irishmen aren't you?

He rubbed his hands and grinned down at the men. He drank in their weakness, eye sockets hollowed and the flesh winnowed on their bones, and he saw too doubt in their eyes that wanted to be assuaged and he pulled at his moustache and put his hands back on his hips.

We are laying the ground for a new kind of engineering. A locomotive line. It's the first of its kind in these parts. I have a contract to fill a valley upon which, when it is done, they will run a locomotive train on top. There is a hill nearby and you will be required to level it for this rail line and then move the land from the hill down into the valley to make the fill. I need the hardiest of the men among you. I will be straight and tell you that the work is tough but it is fine work for strong men such as yourselves. You men will be pioneers and you will build your fortune just like me. I am giving you your start. Those who want to come put up your hands and follow me. I have carts waiting to carry those of you who are coming. I don't need you all mind. If you are bringing with you to America a wife and weans then I don't need you as I can't look after you all. But I wish the best of luck to you. I need single men. Fit and strong.

Some of the men in the crowd began to sidle forward with their families. Duffy watched them go and he eyed up those who remained.

This country is a tough place for men like you, not

knowing a soul in the new world. You can go out there and fend for yerselves but there are all sorts who don't like you, a good many who won't see you as people at all, and what about those shysters and tricksters out there, men who will con you out of what little money you have. Just look at them there behind me waiting to talk to you. He turned as he spoke and reached towards a youth in a sable castor hat fast-talking a family and he yanked him good by the collar till the man came stumbling backwards. This one here, he said, up to no good, and he knocked the man's hat clear with the back of his hand and booted him in the ass. The men laughed and the man hurried after his hat and Duffy looked at the men and smiled voluminously.

You know me boys. I am one of you too. I understand yez. Born and bred in Ulster so I was and I made my way out here as a young man. I'll have you in my care and if you come with me we'll make something of it. I have a house near Chester twenty miles outside the city where you can rest up a few days and we'll begin the start of the week. Fair and honest work. Men of Erin what do you say?

SOON AS I GET PAID I'm gonna get some serious eating done, said The Cutter. His voice heard over the din of the rumbling cart. Drawn faces in front of him, some of them sitting with their arms wrapped around knee-tucked legs and others half standing. He looked at them and licked his lips and smiled. Yessiree. I'm gonna get me a chicken so I am. And I'm gonna get me the hindquarters of a pig and I'm gonna slap them down over a fire. He rubbed his hands.

Are you now, said Coyle.

I am Inishowen.

You must have a wee hunger on you then. I'm gonna get me the whole flank of a cow and I'm gonna eat the whole thing half raw and no one will be getting any of it but meself.

Is that so, said The Cutter.

Aye.

Well you must be eating with the hunger of a wee sparrow for I'm gonna get me a whole cow and a whole pig and a whole clutch of chickens and you can watch me eat em and I'll have the eggs when I'm done. Just for afters.

He spat onto his hands and rubbed them. Across from them sat an old man called Chalky who leaned over and eyed the two men with grim gray eyes. Would yous ever shut your holes, he said.

Deep country for miles on end, fields of wheat and tobacco. They turned off the turnpike and traveled over a pitted dirt track that shook them on top of one another and they elbowed each other in the ribs and arms and laughed. The track opened onto a small valley with a far ravine and they saw the swale was felled of trees, the ancient silence of the place uprooted and a thickening of trees surrounding the valley mute at the spectacle.

The ground was muddied thick despite a scattering of sawdust and they saw a shanty of canvas tents waiting to house them with firepits outside and black cooking pots hanging above them. A low triangle of stacked provisions. Further up the camp they saw horses and mules corralled and the makings of a blacksmith station, wooden huts, carts unhitched and idle, a few men moving about. An air of expectation about the place like the build-up of strange weather. The Cutter walked towards the barrels and squatted down and saw some of them were whiskey. He stood up and kicked a small dance into the air.

Jesus lads, it's fucking Christmas.

IN THE DAYS TO FOLLOW they began to work not like men but beasts. First light of day and they would rise bleary from their tents, their bodies bent and their limbs stiffened and under heavy-lidded eyes their gaze was a distant unseeing. On their faces they wore the land, the earth and the dust embedding their skin and their pallor beneath was gray invisible as it was to the sun and they breakfasted with blackened hands and poured coffee upon tongues parched and whiskey-soured.

The valley surrounding was yellow within green and they would fan up the hill till they looked down upon the swale and they tightened their hands over the hafts of their tools and spat into the dust and they dug. His arms burned and his hands became numb, fingers bloodied and blistered, and every one of the men the same and no one with the intention of relenting. The men worked tireless and unremitting as they pitted the hillside with the points of their picks, the sluggish weight of their tools swung high, the weight stalling sluggish like a pendulum until it was returned hurtling towards the earth, a series of gray comets arcing the sky. The earth crumbled sluggish beneath them, the clod heavy and packed with rotten rock. They burrowed into the surface like animals taking flight from some sluggish danger or as if they were trying to escape the sun's watch, and they worked till the sun drove down weary into the earth, the shadows of the men lengthening before them until each man fell into his own darkness. Upon evening they descended for camp, the earth left open like a raw wound, and they tramped down hungry and sore and they spooned their food onto tin plates by the fire and they drank their whiskey and they gambled and grumbled in the flickering light until like dead men they slept.

Each day anew the sun climbed over the hill and where the earth was rent birdsong died each day. Days of cottoned cloud trapped in the heat and then there were days of clear sky. The sun beat down hard and some men worked without straw hats and others without shirts and he watched the sun work their flesh, whipping skin till it cracked like the beds of rivers strangled.

The stubborn cut hardened its shoulder to the men and the work began to stall. Duffy issued orders and leveled some of them like threats, parading about in palls of blue smoke. The men carted rocks in their hands and Coyle watched Chalky, who some said was near seventy, deliver a stone silent from the earth and shoulder the weight fit for two men on his own with nothing but a suck on his teeth. They carried the stones onto carts alongside shovels of loosened earth and they drove the horse and carts with their timbers trembling down the rugged valley where men made good the fill.

For sups of water they hardly stopped and the stock was better soused and when they did stop for something Duffy's eyes were on them and he made warning to keep working or they would not be paid for the day, for time now was not their own and they learned to watch who was watching and when they stopped to eat they took no more time than was necessary.

Days wore on, time measured by the discordant chimes of the men at their work, seconds clocked by the thudding bluntly of the breaking earth, the clanging of pick on rock. In the valley below they saw the blacksmith hammer and shoe to his own silent beat and he watched them in turn up on the rim scuttling and slaving like ants.

HE BEGAN TO WAKE like he had not slept and all day he craved for sleep. He sat bent upon the fire with few words to go around, supped on his drink and watched the others weighed with the kind of tiredness that pulls a man into the ground. They would eat their fill of potatoes and bread and beans and beef, and the whiskey came easy to their lips. It burned their gullets and eased the pain in their hollowed bodies and made loose their tongues. They talked of the money they would make, farms they would build and the kind of women they would have and he always smiled and laughed with them but inside he saddled his loss. He wondered if the new child had been born, the absent weight of it phantoming into a sorrow that made him weak with frustration and he swore to himself he would get back. Drinking then for there was nothing else to do but salve the day's pain and he listened to the others speak of home and some of them gave song like ghosts breaking free of a bodily burden, and The Cutter spent the time cursing to whoever would listen, that goddamn Duffy, the least he could do is bring us up some fucking hoors, and one by one they fell stiff-backed into sleep.

THEY WATCHED THE MAN slow to a dawdle over his pick. Watched for him too the hawk eyes of Duffy. Knew the man as a quiet one whose laugh was a gassy giggle. They saw his frame sagging and his shoulders shrunk and they knew he was not alright. The man let loose a lethargic swing then let the point of his bedded pick linger and he just stood there a while staring dead at the dirt. Chalky called out to the man and asked if he was alright but the man said nothing and when Chalky called again the man turned his head as if considering a question of great significance but instead he stared back empty.

A tall man with a face banded with dirt came over to him and spoke but the man said nothing to him and the man left and all around the earth shrugged off the men's intrusions. Then the man let drop the tool from his hands and he fell from his feet, fell sullenly like dead meat and lay on his back, and the men watched and when they saw he was not getting up they stopped and bent over him, and they saw his eyes were open and heard him muttering to the sky. I'll kill them all. I'll kill them all so I will.

ANOTHER WEEK OF WORK relentless and the earth bared its teeth as if it was angered at the intrusion. The rock was sheared away in spalls of stone that split the air with no concern for a man's face sending dust that silted their reddened eyes and none of the cutting deep enough despite the calls of Duffy to drive harder. His cigars burned to the butt as he paced in frustration and he cursed the goddamned cut and the useless cunts of Ulstermen and he said they were losing not just days now but weeks.

He disappeared the next morning leaving his deputy in charge, an Irishman called Doyle who carried a heavy foot and kept his face unwashed, the whites of his eyes pure and luminous despite the dust that darkened his face. He ordered the men quietly until a day later Duffy reappeared with men driving horses carting dozens of barrels of black blasting powder while sitting on the back with swinging legs were four face-painted whores.

The men whooped at the sight and that evening they formed brazen queues. Not enough women to go around and only half the men seemed interested anyway, and Coyle watched from the firepit some of the men standing in the queue holding dramatically on to their balls while The Cutter was seen going into the tent twice, and began to queue for a third time until the others protested and a fight ensued.

The next day the women were gone. Near midday the men put down their tools and they left the rock to go below where they watched a group of men begin drilling. They stood atop the rock with hand-held hammers and they beat the bits of the drills into the rock and it dulled their tools and the blacksmith set up station nearby, a man with sorrowful steel eyes and a sad horseshoe moustache, forging and heat-treating and re-sharpening. Eight blast holes were dug and the dusted rock was spooned out and from down below the workers watched the barrels being brought up, the powder poured in and then a group of men set to tamping. A young man called Stamp stood on the ledge with an iron bar in his hand and a pipe in his mouth and he worked the tamping bar downwards. The sun above a burning coin and the men below stood at the water station drinking. Coyle sluiced the brown water over his head and he wiped his eyes and water dribbled off his dusty beard. The Cutter sat down with his head between his legs. He looked up and took his sleeve and wiped snot from his nose and pointed. There's a farm over there on the other side of the valley, he said. Coyle turned his head and wiped water out of his eyes.

Chickens?

Worth a looksee.

The next moment there came an explosion and their hands went to their ears and their bodies cringed instinctively as the sound clattered off the valley. They looked up to see but couldn't see much and they listened incredulous to the rain of rubbled rock. Up on the ridge where Stamp had been standing was now a gout of dark smoke and all about they heard men shrieking. The tampers near him were blown off their feet and they picked themselves up dumbfounded, their hands to their ears as rock hailed all round them. Men below began to rush towards the site and they found Stamp supine, the iron bar three feet long he had been holding blasted clean through the lower flesh of his jaw, up and out through the front of his head, and the bar fell beside a man who stood bleeding, and he picked it up and held it, the item viscid with brain matter, and he looked at the injured man incredulous whose eyes were wide open and his mouth gasping.

There's Duffy, a man said, and they turned to watch the contractor climbing up to the ledge with Doyle dragging behind. He walked towards the men with heated eyes and he stood over Stamp with his hands on his hips and looked down at him and sucked hard on his cigar. The injured man staring blankly at the sky clouding with cigar smoke, his face rock-dusted and unblinking. Another man was bent behind him examining with his hands the hole in the head and Duffy stuck his toe into the man and pointed down into the valley. Take him down to the tent. Jesus. Did I not tell yez no smoking.

When the smoke and dust had cleared a man began to shout and then they found another, a man called Ruddy pinned dead under a rock. He had been blown thirty feet to the other side of the ridge, his legs flattened and a boulder crushing his chest and an eye hanging loose outside his head. The men winced when they saw him and another got sick and two more got iron bars and tried to prise the rock and when that failed they got jacks and worked the boulder free.

In the camp Stamp was alive but by evening he was dead and they made a wooden box for each of the men. They dug a hole in the ground and Duffy looked at it and told them to widen it just in case and they put the coffins in, their feet pointed east and their heads pointing west, and they filled the earth leaving some room beside them. The men asked permission to mourn the dead men and Duffy sucked on his cigar and said you can do whatever you like after dark but it's back to business tomorrow and they went to the shanty and they drank till they slept and in the morning they resumed work, the earth above the dead men unrested.

———————

EACH DAY THE SUN a fury that worked the valley into a dim heat. The cut deepened and in the air the dust hung permanent and one by one the men began to weaken until shadows of men they became. Some of them took injury from falling rocks loosed above them but it was the tiredness that took its toll. He watched a man called Henry drop down beside him, his lips blue and his eyelids brown, and he put a hand over his mouth to see if he was still breathing. He yanked the man up as others gathered round and then Duffy was standing over him.

Coyle motioned towards Duffy. This fella here's sick so he is, he said.

Get you back to work, said Duffy.

This fella needs water.

I won't tell you again.

The Cutter came forward and they dragged the man away to take water and Duffy just stared and then he walked away. The man picked himself up like some elderly convalescent and he took a drink of water in a shaking hand and then he went back to work.

NO WORK ON A SUNDAY and the men lay about the shanty like bovines insensitive, heavy-footed and their eyes dark and their hats hung low. Those that bothered to get up from their beds had cups full of whiskey and they gambled and groused at one another while a man strangled a fiddle till he was told to shut up. A narrow stream ran through the valley and some of them washed their clothes standing naked by the side of it plashing water on their tired bodies.

Coyle gambled with the men and when he lost four dollars he put down his cards and got up. Boys I'm off for a walk. The lingering of a dream in his head and he nosed into the trees, their trunks skinny and snaking skywards and everywhere was green. A dark-eyed junco squatted on a branch near him and he stood and looked at it, never saw a bird like it, and the leaves all around dappled and dazzling in sunlight and he walked up the hill till the sky widened and he saw in the valley below the white spread of a farm. In the lap of a nearby field he could make out two duck-egg-colored carts and he sat and watched the sky broad and blue and he turned and walked back the way he came, inhaling the scent of the forest all the while before he got to the shanty.

He found The Cutter and sat down on a log beside him and took some whiskey in his cup and drank it.

Goddamn rat kept running over me while I was asleep last night, he said.

Some of the men nodded. Aye, said Chalky. Been noticing an increase in them hoors.

When I was a wean, The Cutter said, we used to smoke em out. We'd plug up all the holes but for one and then we'd light a wee fire and the rats would all come running out, hundreds of them, and we'd have the dogs there waiting. The dogs went wild so they did.

Some of the men laughed. A man staggered over from a circle of gamblers and he took out his cock and began to piss in front of them. The Cutter looked up. Are ye making me a proposition?

The man's eyes slanted. What?

Would you ever fuck off with that skinny thing and go an piss someplace else.

I'm pissin here so I am.

Coyle stood up and went to the man and pushed him hard with the flat of his hand in the face. The man staggered till he fell over on his back and a dark stain began to spread on his leg and some of the men laughed and others let out a cheer. Coyle sat back down on the log and the man picked himself up and he stared at Coyle before stumbling away.

That'll learn ye, The Cutter said.

Coyle took a stick and began to scratch with it odd shapes in the ground like he was trying to divine the runes of some obscure language housed within him.

TWO DAYS LATER CAME first rain. He watched the sky swell and roll darkly over the valleys and he whispered to himself, make it come. Cloud shadow darkened the swirling dust and the sky thundered above them. Then it came, rain thick and pounding, spilled as if burst from a belly, and the men stopped their work. Some of them took off their hats and arced their faces and opened their mouths and some of them smiled and light returned to their eyes, narrow smiles of happiness but inside them a turmoil of sadness that bestowed on them again their humanity. Two young men began to wrestle with each other, a hand on each other's collar and they went down to the ground laughing. Duffy watched the men from above on his horse and he looked up at the sky and he turned and rode away to the trees. The Cutter put down his pick and began to take off his clothes. He appointed his mouth like a stoup to receive the rain and he peeled his tattered garments, rumbles of laughter from his dirty black chest and naked in the puddling dust he lay. Coyle smiled and sat on a rock and he looked at an embankment of cloud. It reached down to meet the hills and he saw the ground beneath his boots soften, watched it receive the rain until it began to wear, drop by drop, and the ground was no longer what it was and began to wash away and he had the thought that all of life in the end was like this.

The Cutter stood up and his body began to shake and Coyle saw he was starting to dance, his knees furling and his elbows taking wing till he was caught up in the fury of some demented jig, the melody and cadence of which were known only to his inner self, and he was howling and the others began to watch and struck by it too they began to strip, peeling their clothes until they were revealed in their nakedness, soiled and sodden and they linked their arms and they kicked their feet into the air and they danced and they danced and they danced.

THAT DAY OF RAIN was singular and the days warmed again. The land returned to dust and in the valley below the fill became a minor hill, rising imperceptibly at first over the stone culvert, then reaching slowly towards the leafy shoulders of the valley. Heat from the sky and heat from the earth and one by one on the valley floor the horses and mules began to fall. They would sink to their knees and lie down still, eyes glossed and distant. The men would holler and boot them in the ribs but the animals looked back with eyes that spoke a singular language understood by the men. Each animal was shot and its corpse dragged away and its meat when it could be eaten was butchered and cut to shreds and jerked.

He bent to the ground and broke it with his pick and he came back up and saw his father backbent and brushing smooth the sable flank of a horse. Here gimme that. The man pointing to the dandy brush.

Again, loping up the road, the dog circling and nosing his heels. Long legs and the sky low as if it were coming down to meet him and his father not bothered by the rain. Never was. You're as soon as wet as you're dry again and you're as soon as dry as wet again. No point fighting it.

After the rain the world glossed new and the air smelling damply.

——————————

THEY SAW IN THE NEAR dark the stranger had more teeth missing than remaining and he eyed up the men with the giddy look of a hemmed-in hound let loose. When he spoke they figured him for a fool, his voice taking flight with rampant enthusiasm though he was an Irishman like all of them and so they took to him and they asked him what part he was from. He told them he was from Kerry and he had come from the canal digs, walked some forty miles finding food just the twice and he had to steal it once from a dog and the dog wasn't too happy about it and another time he had to go into a house but fuck them. There were terrible things he had to get away from but the weather was nice and sure it wasn't too bad sleeping outdoors though it was a bit cold aye at night and that's all there was to it. Here I am, Maurice is the name, two shites and a shovel. When he spoke he looked about the ground as if he were looking for something he dropped and when he finished they saw he was eyeing up the stew in the firepit.

What kind a things are you talking about? said Chalky.

Sickness, Maurice said. They got it bad. But I ain't hanging about to get it for no man so I'm not. I've been walking for three days. Wild arse burn on me so I have now gimme a hanch of that supper. He produced a tin plate from the backseat of his pants and pitched it forward in front of him. Two shites and a shovel, he said.

PINK LIPS LAUGHING on the black faces of the men when they saw the fella slink off to the woods assclutching. A bony kid called Glacken and he stayed there for hours and they became grim-faced when he returned and went to the ground and did not get up. Two of the men carried him to the shanty. He groaned throughout the night and in the morning his face was puckered and his eyes were sunken glass and he gasped for water and the men gave it to him but the kid found no relief. Duffy came to look and he told the men to clear a tent for the kid and they put him in there shivering and stomach-clutching, for what Duffy feared most he had seen evident in the symptoms of the man. The workers asked if he would spare one of them to stay, for the kid needed nursing, but Duffy said he would not and it would do neither him nor them any good at all and they left Glacken in the morning to his moaning.

During the day the blacksmith looked in on him, fetched water in a bucket and fed it to him and when darkness fell they returned to the shanty and found the kid worse and later that night one of the men noticed he was dead. Another man started shitting badly and he came back saying he was sick and then he was taken to the tent. In the morning Coyle and The Cutter went with two others to dig a hole. They put the body in a wooden box and buried him and when they were finished and standing over the grave they saw Doyle dragging his heavy foot up the fill towards them. He came near and stopped and looked at them with white ringing eyes and pointed to them. The four of yous. Come with me. The men looked at each other and followed him down to the sheds where he started hitching horses. I need yous to go on these carts with me into Philly for supplies.

THE CARTS WERE LOADED with boxes of goods that reached up near five feet to the heavens and then the men tied tarpaulin on top. Doyle appeared out of the back of a building scanning as he walked a pocket watch. I've got to go and find some folk, he said. It might take me a few hours so hold on till I be back. He looked about for where he left his hat and found it resting nearby on a barrel and he set off limping out past the gate. Coyle sat up on the edge of a cart kicking the air while the others sat on the ground. I'm famished, he said.

The Cutter turned towards him. Aye. And I need to be slaked. He rubbed his hands and looked towards the other two men. Yous aren't sitting about here like fools when there's a wee sup to be had?

One of the men frowned and looked about over his shoulder towards the other man who was silent. Naw. I'm waiting here so I am.

The Cutter shook his head at them. I am in me hole. We'll be back before him. Come on Inishowen.

The Cutter turned and paraded towards the gate and Coyle shouted after him. Will ya hold on a minute till we figure where we're going.

The Cutter bellowed over his shoulder. Fuck knows, he said and he disappeared out the gate.

AFTERNOON SUN SHOT fire through the Philadelphia streets. Coyle and The Cutter wandered the alien thoroughfares, jostled in the mud tracks by a clamor of bodies, the calls of bootboys with blackened faces and butchers bloodied, and they stared at the faces of negro men, complexions that were unknown to them. Everywhere signs for objects for sale and the invitations of merchant men marshalling prospectors to their wares, their voices fat with bombast masking thin desperation and the two men pressed their noses at shop fronts full of fancy items they knew not what they were for. Women haranguing over handcarts and the better-dressed in ribbon and colorful cloaks and they watched wealthy men smart-dressed and striding, each one they stared at in his finery though they learned their gaze was invisible.

Music jingling and jaunting towards them and they came upon a man with jesting eyes and a grease-painted moustache winding a barrel organ. On a string was tied a miniature monkey and it held out a tiny hat and the men stared at the creature incredulous and they asked the winder what it was and he looked at them puzzled and he told them to speak in English and they winced at him and said they were and walked on.

They were tired and they licked their dry lips and they decided they wanted a drink. A place signed Bull's Head Tavern and they opened tentatively the door. Card players with clean faces and suits and they stopped their game to eye the two strangers. A man coughed and they thought they heard him say dirty Irish and they felt they were being watched. The Cutter clanked coins on the counter and waved a grubby hand and ordered two drinks but the barman turned away from them. The Cutter spoke again but was met by silence and he slammed his fist on the counter. I got fucking money don't I? he said and a white-suited man with an ivory-handled cane stood tall from a table and Coyle pulled The Cutter by the sleeve and yanked him till they were outside.

They walked through tapering streets where the sun did not reach. Children playing in the dirt with dogs and pigs grunting and women standing about talking with faces sober and skeletal. They recognized the Delaware and the waterfront opened up to them, the bowsprits of the ships stretching forward to poke windows. Coyle nodded towards a small tavern and they went to it and hesitated at the door and they went to the window and peered in. Go on, The Cutter said. The door thirsty on its hinges and the place quarter full, stevedores and sailors and stewbums drinking under a stuttering lamp. The room was sliced by window light and the wooden beams creaked under their feet and no one looked up. A barman lifted himself up weary from a stool and they took to a corner where the light had receded and was cool. They lined two ales in front of them and two shots of whiskey and they crossed the beer through the other's arms and put the glasses to their lips and drained them. The beer beaded their chins and they washed their whiskeys down on the second breath and Coyle ordered another round. The barman winced at him through eyes shot with red lightning and he took the money and shuffled to their drinks.

They slouched on wooden chairs the way of old men with bones tired from too much living. Coyle picked at the calluses on his hands and he watched a bluebottle flit their glasses of beer. A man groped a woman in a corner and she giggled at his touch and The Cutter watched them and then he stood with a dirty grin. Back in a bit.

Coyle supped his beer and looked at the others, men with stone faces and powerful arms tattooed an elaborate dark green, and a gangly kid came from a back door carrying a block of sweating ice. The barman nodded to the kid and took a pick and began chipping at it. The door creaked open and The Cutter beamed in ushering two women ahead of him. The women nodded to the barkeeper and the barkeeper nodded back and the women smiled at Coyle and The Cutter sat them down at the table.

This here's Daisy and this here's June. Or is it the other way round?

They each wore a calico dress one red and one black and they wore satin hats and June the taller of them had painted her lips garish and he watched her and saw through her forced smile.

This man here's looking forward to meetin you, The Cutter said.

Coyle smiled. Surely.

The Cutter stood to the bar and ordered a round for all four and the door opened and two men walked in. The Cutter sat down and began to talk to the women when he heard an Irish accent behind him. He turned around and then he saw who it was. He turned back quick and then snuck another look and he leaned over to Coyle and whispered. There's a dead man standing at that bar.

Coyle looked up and saw the backs of two men and he shrugged in disappointment. The Cutter turned around and saw the men standing with their drinks. One of them spun a coin with a grubby thumb on the counter and he was chatting to the barman. The other then turned and he locked eyes with Coyle. The Mute. The eyes of the man gave a startle and then they went mean and he held his stare with Coyle till he put down his drink and walked out.

Coyle stood up. How the fuck?

It wasn't surely.

It was.

He must have swam for it.

But I thought—

They looked towards the man keeping the company of The Mute but he turned too and went out.

Well huppidy hah, Coyle said.

They drank their whiskey and they ordered two more beers and the women slouched and fanned their faces and one of them passed a vanity mirror to the other and the men told them stories to which only they laughed and the women smiled and when they had finished their drinks they looked at each other and asked the men if they were ready. They stood up for outside. At the end of the street a dark-lit hotel, the paint peeling and a sign for vacancies on the door and the man at the counter just nodded.

Their clothes were black and stuck to their skin and they peeled them off and stood black-toed in front of each other laughing.

You look like one of them nigger fellas.

You're as black as the divil's cock.

The women steered them to a basin and pitcher and they too began to undress.

CRAWLING SHADOWS on the streets. The Mute walked with his shoulders hunched and he heard steps coming behind him. He drew a knife and turned quick for confrontation and then he saw it was his friend. He scowled and turned back and walked on ignoring the chasing steps of the man. The friend caught up, chin-bearded and breathless, and he pulled at The Mute in protest, asked him with cobalt eyes shining what was going on but The Mute just shook him off and pointed. They crossed a network of cramped side streets and stepped out onto a boulevard. The Mute threaded the hackney cabs and coaches and he found the steps of the Walnut House Hotel on the other side of the street. The building three stories in white and The Mute walked up to the front doors and he turned and waited for his companion and then they went in.

Shadows leaned on the street like vagrants waiting for the night. Lamps flared and a piano pealed and a gray cat prowled and stretched. The doors of the hotel opened and The Mute and his friend walked out. They stood on the steps with their hands awkward in their pockets. The companion pulled the hair on his chin and he looked to The Mute who shrugged his shoulders and turned and watched the front door. He walked onto the street and scuffed the pavement with the toe of his boot and then the door opened. The single eye of Macken and the man buttoning a long coat and behind him striding through the doors came the great height of Faller. He looked down at the young man and then turned to Macken.

Pay him, he said. But if you're lying to me Mute you know that I'm going to take more than my money back.

THE MUTE AND HIS FRIEND led the men to the dram house and they stood on the opposite corner and watched. Faller and Macken crossed the street and unbuttoned their coats and stood outside the bar and then went inside. The Mute swallowed and he hitched up his collar and he looked to his friend. The mewling of a child down the street and they heard a man approach and they watched him go past. He stopped when he saw them, a wild-eyed idiot of a man and stinking. He held out a hand gnarled and brown and he smiled sweetly like a child to the men. The Mute leaned out and kicked the air in front of him and the bum made a quick retreat and scampered around the corner. Across from them the door of the dram house opened. Yellow light leaned out onto the street and Faller and Macken emerged. The barkeeper came with them and he hung on the jambs and pointed to a hotel down the street. The Mute watched Faller tip his hat in thanks and begin to walk towards it.

FALLER STEPPED INTO the hotel with Macken behind him and he saw the administrator's desk and a man behind it. The man was bald with sagging jowls and he licked his lips with a lazy gray tongue. Faller smiled and tipped his stovepipe hat.

I believe you have a man inside paying time to be with a woman whom I really must see.

The man looked at Faller and arched an eyebrow.

The man or the woman?

The man.

I'm afraid I can't.

Faller smiled and leaned over the desk interrupting. Right now.

He leaned back and fluttered his jacket to reveal the silver of his gun. The man looked at the weapon and his breath held still and he surveyed Macken behind.

I don't want no shooting in my hotel, he said. Top floor. Room number fifteen. No dirty business mind. You can take it outside.

Faller tipped his hat and smiled. Macken already on the stairs. They approached the landing on the third floor and looked left then stepped right and went quietly down the corridor. Their breaths held and the tock of a grandfather clock all there was to be heard but for the faint creak of the wooden slats and then further still a faint moaning. A door with the number fifteen peeling off it and they stood and listened. Macken looked at him and questioned with his eyebrow and Faller nodded him towards the door. Macken leaned back and kicked it and the lock shuddered but held and he kicked it quickly again. Wood fractured and the door swung open and he charged in with his gun pointed ahead of him, the bed behind the door, and he saw a man portly and middle-aged rolling away naked. A woman on her knees with her wrists tied to the brass and she looked up and began to scream and the man saw the intruder's gun and his hand was already under the pillow and upon a revolver which he cocked in fluid motion. He swung up and around, his chest a swirl of matted gray hair and the legs of the woman kicking, and he lifted his gun and fired at the stranger. The door splintered by Macken's head and he ducked and returned a shot. When he looked up he saw the man was on the floor, the bullet passed clean through his neck to sit snug in the wall. Faller stepped in and he looked at the man on the floor slumped with a hand to his throat and heard the sound of the man gurgling.

A connecting door between the two rooms and Coyle bent down to the keyhole. He came back up his face bleached white and he jabbed his finger in the air towards the window.

Run.

The two women sat up on the beds with alarm wild in their eyes and in the adjoining room the woman was still screaming. Faller went to her and smacked her on the ass and when she did not stop he leaned down to her and lifted her by the hair and told her to be quiet and the whimpering stopped. He turned towards the window, the light crepuscular, and he witnessed Coyle, the man hanging in a blue-skinned suit of nakedness from a low roof and then dropping onto the street and another man handing him a bundle and Faller straightened and leaned back and he kicked open the window. He was too big to climb out of it and by then the men were gone and he glared at Macken and went into the next room cursing.

FALLER LIFTED A WORN wooden chair resting by the wall and he put it down by the beds. The chair creaked when he sat on it and he leaned back and drew his double-barreled gun. He put it on his lap then reached into his shirt pocket and he took out his pipe. He told the two women to put on their clothes and they stood off the beds unashamed and began to dress. Faller watched them, filling his pipe with tobacco from a tin and then he lit it and told the women to sit down. They looked at each other nervously and sat together on the bed and Macken fidgeted by the door. He swung his neck out upon the hall and looked back in. We'd better get going, he said.

Faller turned his head to the man and said nothing.

I'm just saying, said Macken. He came back into the room and fidgeted and looked at the girls and he went to the window and ran his hand over his belt and gun. Faller turned in the chair and faced the women. From the front of the hotel there came the sound of men's voices growing urgent in the street. The women looked at Faller and they looked at his gun pregnant on his lap and they saw the ornamentation on it, the curlicued designs, and they grew afraid. He smiled. Ladies. You will tell me about those two gentlemen and then I will let you go.

The women looked at each other. June reapplied her face paint and spoke with fresh crimson lips that she puckered to Faller invitingly. I don't know nothing about them other than they're filthy and they're Irish. A quick sharp laugh slipped out of her red mouth but when she saw Faller's face impassive she caught it.

And where do you figure then they're to be found?

The woman shrugged.

You don't know, Faller said. He drew on his pipe and blew smoke in their faces. The other woman spoke. They're railway boys. They said they were digging the railways. One of them said they were digging for an Irishman and they were going back this evening.

Faller smiled and then he stood up. That was easy wasn't it? he said. The women smiled and made to get up with their belongings.

Not yet.

Outside a man's voice was echoing excitedly in the street. Faller belted his gun and leaned slowly towards the two women and put his huge hands softly to their necks. Daisy smiled coquettish and June shifted on her seat and he looked at her a moment, stared deep into the plunging sea of her eyes. A malevolence then she saw in the way he looked at her and she flinched and scratched him. He shifted back and then he tightened his grip, watched her pupils dilate and the women began to kick their legs, recoiling uselessly from the size of the man. Macken coughed and he said in a low voice there's no need and Faller ignored him, just stared, the women's mouths gaping and their skin turning ashen, and Macken said again louder this time will you stop and the women began to cease kicking and their bodies went limp and Faller released them onto the bed. Macken stood and stared open-mouthed at the bodies and began mumbling and Faller turned and walked serene from the room ducking his head under the door. They descended the stairs towards the waiting men who formed a block in the foyer by the door and then the men parted when Faller opened his coat to show he was armed and he passed through them smiling.

THEY RAN NAKED through the city. Darkness was closing in on them and their clothes and boots were bundled in their arms and soon they were blind to their bearings. In horror they were witnessed by a pair of bonneted women who had stepped out of a house and who returned indoors at the sight of them. Coyle stubbed a toe and began to hobble. He cursed and came to a stop and began to walk with a limp and they found a dark alley. The men were panting and their flesh was a plucked-hide pimpling and the alley stank of rotting fish and ammonia and they got down quietly on their haunches. They felt through their clothes and figured them out in the dark and began to put them on. Coyle stuck out his feet and booted them and winced when he stood on his toe. He poked his head out around the corner watching. Nothing save the nosing of a pair of scruff dogs.

He slipped back down again and whispered. I figure we lost him.

The Cutter whispered angry. Who in the hell did we lose?

His name's Faller.

Is that who you were running from back home?

Aye.

Thought as much. What's he doing here then?

Come for me so he has.

Ye must have annoyed him.

Coyle said nothing and kept watch around the corner. The Cutter tapped him on the shoulder.

What was he doing then shooting a gun in the other room?

Fuck do I know. Coyle rubbed his face and sat thinking a moment. Maybe he thought it was me.

We'd better get back to Doyle and the others or we'll be left behind.

We've already missed em.

The Cutter spat onto the ground. Fuck it.

They stood up and walked out onto the street and they ran down another and then they began to walk.

This toe of mine is busted.

What'd you do that this fella wants you so bad?

I didn't give him the satisfaction of getting caught.

The streets began to square off neatly and they found themselves in the city's better parts. No lamplight to be seen and not a soul on the streets, the busy thorough-fares of the day swallowed by darkness. Their guide was the moonlight and it beamed down full on top of them and there was occasional light from the windows of hotels. Under the shop awnings a darkness more compact and they walked with the aid of it, not a word between them and their eyes watched over their backs all the while. Not a murmur of the wind nor a turning of a wheel and the only sounds were their footsteps.

They came to a marble building grand and silent and they recognized it as a place they had been earlier that day and they worked out where they were from it. The night sky was clear and their minds were alert and they had figured how to get out of the city. They heard the approaching clatter of a horse and buggy of some kind and it came from the shadows and passed before them a darkly specter with no persons visible. They stopped at a trough and cupped horse water into their mouths and Coyle took off his boot and rubbed his toe and dipped it in the water.

Along the margins of the road they walked or they rimmed the edges of ripening fields, crops tipping blue in the moonlight, and they kept steady watch behind them. The air was warm and meshed with the chorus of cicadas that made the air dense and unnerving. Each man eaten up by fear and The Cutter felt better for talk.

We must be safe now, he said.

I think I have to go, said Coyle.

What do you mean?

I have to leave.

Leave where?

Away from here. The cut. He'll find me and I donny want no harm coming to you. I've caused enough of it.

I donny think he'll find you out there.

I think before another day is done I'll be found surely and he'll be done with me. He's wise in the way of killing in ways that we are not and I've had more luck than any man. The strange thing is I can deal with that. You know, I want to stop running. I'm tired of it. My bones are telling me they're done. And part of me even wants to go back. How strange is that? It's not that I'm afraid of what's coming to me because I donny think I can stop it. I believed I had done good in escaping him and now it seems I have not. And yet the one reason I have to go on is I'm afraid for my children. I reckon the other one's born now and there's a strange power in me that makes me want to go on for them despite myself. I feel I owe it to them though I donny know how or what.

The Cutter looked at him and said nothing.

A SUN ROLLED RED over the low black hills clotting the sky with light. The shadows shied away to reveal fields of wheat and they walked in that dawn light sensing they had drawn near to Duffy's cut. They saw a farmstead flash golden in the lee of a hill and they approached it, climbed over a fence and waded through a field of corn, The Cutter snatching at a sheaf and they heard a dog barking. It came towards them and stopped at the perimeter of the yard snouting the air with a barrage of sharp barks and then it lowered its head to look at them. The collie furred in mustard and coal and about the ears some cream and The Cutter whistled and bent down to it. The dog eyed him suspiciously then wagged its tail and came towards him and he took the dog and rolled it sideways rumpling its ears.

A cart asleep in the yard and they went around the back to the door and they knocked. Lamplight leaked underneath and it softened the ground under the window and they heard the scrawk of a chair and then footsteps coming towards them. A woman. Her head in a shawl and her hands floured and she held open the door with her foot. The men nodded politely and they asked please for a drink of water and a bite of something to eat, said they had been traveling all night, and they saw the eyes of the woman as she took them in head to toe and then she stared at the dog and went inside. They stood waiting and The Cutter rubbed his hands and hung out his tongue in expectation and he bent to the dog and ruffed it. The door pulled open and they saw a balding man with red cheeks pointing a rifle out the door towards them. He shook the gun upwards into the air. This here's private property now git off it.

The men put their hands in the air and said they meant no harm but were hungry that's all and they saw the peering eyes of children through a triangle of legs. They backpedaled slowly till there was distance enough to turn and they ran down a dirt track away from the house. They joined up with the road and they were sullen and silent and they passed other farmhouses brightening in the morning light but they stayed away, their feet sore as hell and west they continued to walk.

THEY ROSE AT DAWN and left the hotel without eating, the streets dewed silver as the thoroughfares quivered to life. They turned where the shadows lingered plum on the side streets and came to an alley that led to a black door and Faller knocked three times. The door gave a short squeal and before them hunched a man with yellow whiskers. He had two eyes each different from the other, one ash and the other steel, and he looked up inquisitive at Faller.

You Hardy? Faller said.

You here for horses? the man said.

Faller nodded. The man motioned them through the door. Cmon then.

They walked through the house, the place dim and damp and buzzing with flies, and there was somebody else sitting quietly in shadow. They came to another door that opened upon a yard. The light in the stable was low and the man lit a lamp and passed it looking upwards at Faller and he watched the tall man begin to examine the animals.

The lot of them are neutered cept for that mare of course there, he said pointing.

Macken turned to him. We'll be needing gear as well, oilskins too if you have them.

The man nodded. I git everything you need.

He looked sideways at the men and figured they were carrying guns but pretended to pay no attention. Faller pointed to the chestnut mare and a black gelding and the man rubbed his hands and nodded approval.

How much? Faller said.

The man scratched his face. Let's see all you need first.

They loaded the horses and took them to a rusted trough to drink, the water filmed with a faint rainbow of oil, and they guided them out onto the street. They rode free of the city, past houses pillared proud and white, and gradually they entered wide country. Red-roofed farms blazed the countryside among great wheat fields and pasture sloped with inky cattle that watched the riders blankly. The sun was hot and they took off their jackets and they slugged water from their flasks. Macken coughed into his fist and he cleared his throat and he looked at Faller and he looked away again.

There was no need for that, he said.

Faller looked at him. No need for what?

That. Last night. Them two girls. They done nothin.

Everybody's done something, Faller said. It's just a case of who decides.

That don't make it right.

Faller screwed tight his flask and put it back in its holding.

Weight. That I believe is the problem.

Huh?

I said the problem is that of weight. Think about it.

He looked at Macken, who looked back at him, his face scrunched in confusion.

A child in the womb lives in warmth without weight. And then it is born and it becomes this mewling thing, like an animal. Did you ever wonder about that Macken? Why this is so? It is because it feels itself for the first time, discovers its own weight in the world. And it comes as a shock to it. Never really gets over it. With weight comes sensation and pain and hunger and the need for sleep and all these wants and needs and all of that ad infinitum.

What's that got to do with anything?

You see, the child never recovers from the pain of its own weight. It grows and as it does so it needs and wants more. Always more, never less. All that insatiable hunger for things. Give a hungry man soup and he asks for meat. And when he's given meat one finds he's sitting at your table. Next thing he's asking for the silverware. You really do have to think about that. Every desire a man has that is satisfied leads to a new one. It's an unstoppable thing, the boundlessness of it, desire always hovering beyond man's grasp.

Faller kicked his horse forward and Macken rode alongside him, his face puzzling and then it straightened. People are still people though, most of the time, he said.

Let me tell you something Macken. People aren't people. They are animals, brutes, blind and stupid following endless needs they know not of what origin. And all the rest that we place on top to make us feel better is a delusion. The price of life is the burden of your own weight and some people are better off without it.

MID-MORNING AND A MEADOW full of fruit. They climbed over a fence and entered wary watching like dogs. He picked a peach and slathered over it, teeth like fangs, and he punctured its flesh and it gave up its moisture to him, trickled off his lips, was sweet to the tongue. The Cutter bent to the ground and raised two fallen peaches, rubbed their bruised flesh with his thumb, and they sucked on the husks till they were dry as stones, both of them silent, and they walked to a cluster of trees that blushed with glossy apples and they filled their pockets with them.

Deep ache in their legs. They took rest under the abundance of an oak and Coyle rubbed his toe and they reckoned they were close to the dig. They leaned back onto the blue-shadowed grass, gurgle of brook and the breathy whisper of leaves and one after the other they fell asleep. A warbler wasp-colored took to a branch above them and shook it with its weight and it whistled while the sun fought a finger of cloud and rolled free. Wind shook the grass. Coyle awoke softly riding on the momentum of sleep. The face of his daughter and the peach smell of her flesh and when clarity seized his mind he stood up with a strange feeling and put his hand in his pocket and realized the ribbon was gone.

THE CUTTER LOOKED at him, his face gurning with disdain, his yellow teeth bared, and then he scratched the gray of his jaw. Like fuck we're going back.

Coyle did not answer him, just stared him long in the eye. The Cutter stared him right back, saw the man was not going to be stared down. Ye must be mental.

Coyle turned and went to the fence and scaled it quickly for the road. An apple in The Cutter's hand and his knuckles tightened white around it and he hurled it at the oak tree, the fruit shattering, and then he began to follow. Arrah fuck.

Coyle walking with his eyes on the road and The Cutter came alongside him muttering. A bloody ribbon what in the hell.

Coyle answered without lifting his head. I had it in my hand only a wee while ago. It'll have to be about.

They took the narrow road between them, a hill rising languorous before them and the road indented with the dry markings of cartwheels baked by the sun. Coyle nudged the fringe grass with his foot while a red-tailed hawk wheeled the air above them, found shapes of air invisible to glide on.

He could feel his heart seize tight. He walked holding his breath, balling his fists and cracking his knuckles, and he began to feel a sadness he could not control as if more weight had been dropped on top of him. A knot began to stone in his stomach until it was big enough to burst him. Nothing but a fool so I am. One wee thing I had left and now I've gone and lost her.

They came to the top of the hill, two pillar forms under vast sky, and they saw the expanse of land spread out around them, serried green corn wagging in the breeze and in the distance the blood roof of a barn. He saw The Cutter bend to his shoelace and he was watching idly the road's distant tapering when he saw them. A trembling at the far length of the road. The fleet shadows of horses. He reached for words in his throat but could not get a hold of them and The Cutter without turning seemed to smell the trouble off him and when he stood and saw the horses he too was ashen for he knew then that they were visible.

They turned and began to run down the hill, swift past the orchard, and The Cutter ahead of him and he heard the man roar out at him to leap into the corn. The Cutter then was gone, into the grasp of the field over the leaning beams of a fence, and he followed the man's heels, was upon the fence and the wood decrepit and it collapsed under him. He fell on his back staring up at the road, the cottoned blue sky, the silence of the place but for the thumping of his heart, and he picked himself up winded and pushed in.

He could hear it behind him. The commotion of horse hoofs pounding the road. The silence of them coming to a stop and then the shouting of men. The swish and snap of corn and The Cutter just in sight and then there was a voice shouting behind him. One step further into that field and I'll blow your heads clean off ya.

THE MEN TOOK THEM out onto the road and circled them.

Sit down there on the ground.

The nose of a shotgun looking down at him and a man leaning behind it.

Three men in black beaver hats, two of them with guns and their horses behind them, and he saw in one of them the red-cheeked face of the farmer from earlier that morning. The man held the gun with fat pink fingers and he looked at them nervously. The Cutter looked up at them incredulous and then he found his voice. Who are yous?

Shut up.

The man standing in front had a jutting brown beard and was the elder of the three and he nodded to the man who spoke. We're the local horse company and it's our business to keep out any trouble. Right now you'uns is trespassing.

He directed them with his gun to get up. Coyle and The Cutter stood uneasily to their feet and put their hands into the air over their heads.

Are yous railway Irish?

Trying to get back so we are.

We don't want your lot around here. Which mile were yous working?

Mile fifty-nine.

What's that ye say?

I said fifty-nine. Duffy's cut.

One of the men whispered to another and they looked at the men.

What's that in yer pockets? The man nodded towards their trousers.

Just fruit is all.

Them's not your fruit. Give em here.

The men emptied their pockets and handed the fruit over and the men took the fruit and realized they did not know what to do with them. The bearded man motioned with his gun again.

Git walking. Up thataways. He pointed to the road. Coyle took a step forward and The Cutter was slow to move and one of them prodded him in the shoulder with the gun. The Cutter turned and stared hard at the man. Be my pleasure, the man said and the third man cocked his rifle. The Cutter walked on. The men mounted their horses and followed closequarters.

Not a word as they walked and the horsemen behind them kept their counsel but for the bearded one who spoke to give the walkers directions. The land turned pale and it began to drizzle and the horsemen sheathed themselves in skins and the two men walked feeling glad for the cooling rain. A farmstead broke the rise of a low hill and they saw two blond boys being circled in a field by a dog. The children stopped as the men on the road neared and they went to the fence to watch the gunpoint procession. The Cutter winked at them as the dog stood wagging its tail and they looked towards the horsemen uncertainly and ran away.

They passed workers bent in fields who stood to watch them passing, some of them shielding the sun from their eyes and some of them waving at the gunmen. Two of them came to a fence and a member of the gun party went down to talk to them.

A different road around noon and they recognized the looming shape of the valley. They followed the track towards the site where the cut was teeming and the men went to the shanty with the horsemen behind them and they stopped at the water station to get a drink. The bearded man left the group and nosed about on his horse looking for the foreman and he stopped and watched as two men carried the body of a choleric man from the mouth of a tent, the dead man's head bloated and loose off his shoulder, and the horseman blessed himself and he reversed his animal with dread, turned with a sharp pull of the reins and went back to the others pointing. He told the men what he saw and their minds went wild with the thought of disease and they put their sleeves to their mouths to protect them from the air and they turned their horses one-handed and fled.

———————

THE TRACK BOBBED UP and then the land leaned down to reveal clusters of green. Thick trees knotting the horizon in darker myrtle and nearby ran a small brook. Faller rode ahead in rigid right-angle with a survey map in hand while Macken was silent and slanting. They went to the stream and dismounted, the water bubbling into their bottles and they drank it rusty red. They led the horses back onto the track and Faller stopped and stood still. Wait, he said. He looked at the sky and studied the land from where they had traveled and then he lit his pipe. Blue smoke coiled as he sucked on the stem and then he turned and remounted. The horses trotted on towards a hillock and they came to a cleft of rock bucked like two front teeth and they rode slowly downwards. Clear blue sky ahead of them and from the east a roiling of gray and Faller began to slow down till he was alongside Macken.

We're being followed, he said.

He spoke without turning but Macken stirred as if he had just been kicked and he leaned around to look, squinted single-eyed at the haze of green and turned around again.

I don't see nobody.

Faller sucked on his pipe and rubbed slowly his moustache. They're keeping distance. That alone makes it more interesting.

How'd you figure?

I wonder now who they are.

Faller nudged the chestnut mare ahead of Macken in an easy four-beat gait and Macken followed with his head craning over his shoulder.

It'd be better if you would not let them know we know, Faller said.

What do you reckon they're going to do?

Faller did not bother to answer. Macken held the reins in his left hand and he checked the gun in his belt with the right and he looked to the butt of the rifle diagonal on the horse in its scabbard.

The land rolled in patches of umber and it lay uneven around them, fields of leaning wheat and tobacco greening, and Faller took out the map again and examined it and pointed. Town this way. The mouth of a valley loomed and widened and they ambled up a hill gently, trees a medley of green under a cobalt sky smeared white. They rode through woodland, the trees thickening in conspiracy and bird call rattling and Faller slowed the horse till it seemed he wanted to travel at no speed at all and Macken grew agitated behind him. The forest cleared and a farmhouse sat among an apron of fields. They met an old man along the edge of a field, his clothes a patchwork of seasoned mendings, and he watched them with gimlet eyes as they approached. He nodded and they nodded in return and Macken stopped just as he was past him and asked if he knew where the railway digs were to be found. Take yer pick, the man said. A belt of gray stubble on his face and he wagged a scrawny finger wide. There's digs all about these townships over there.

Faller motioned for Macken to go on and when he reached him he stared at him. Why are you telling others our business?

I was just wondering.

Keep our business to ourselves till I figure out who is following.

They rode slow again till Macken complained they'd be quicker walking on foot and Faller said nothing and then he said their followers didn't want to be drawn out. They took a horse-beaten track and it led them to the shape of a village and on the outskirts they found a lumber tavern. They stopped at the lean-to and dismounted and tied their horses and they went inside where they were met by a gray-haired woman in gingham. She stood to them sideways and took them to a room at Faller's instruction that watched out onto the street and when the woman turned to leave he saw a goiter in her throat like a fist.

Faller took his gun and put it on his lap and he sat on a chair at the open window. Macken went downstairs and he asked for food and had it sent up. They sat slurping their beef stew in bowls with their eyes watching. The lace curtain danced ghostly in the breeze. After some time two young men on horses ambled through and Macken stiffened straight. That them do you reckon?

Faller shook his head. You'll know.

THE MEN RETURNED to the dig and the others gave a round of applause and they bent smiling to receive it. I'm docking yous boys a morning's pay, Duffy said and they were expecting more but that was all of it. They took to work like before and a brief shower of rain fell and it cooled their working bodies. It moistened the open ground and he smelt the raw earth. He watched a raven swoop down low over them, a yelp like a sob from its beak, and the way it glided on the warm air. And then it swooped down into the valley where ten men had taken ill. Their bodies were spent from the violence of voiding, lying as they did in their own excrement and vomit, and they were dehydrated from their efforts and calling for water. Doyle had brought back with him four Sisters of Charity, feetless scuttling apparitions shrouded in black with cornets white-winged who took to minding the men, worked without word between them as they went to the water station and began to wash some of the sick men and they were watched by the others who fought feelings of both horror and comfort.

Coyle rammed the pick into the earth and turned to The Cutter.

I'm going off so I am.

Whereabouts?

He looked across the valley where the horizon met

distant green. Dunno yet. Far. Gonna try going back.
You know how it is.

When are you going?

Soon as I can get paid next.

Would you not go as it is?

I can't. I left the last of it in that hotel room.

The Cutter looked at him.

No point going nowhere with no money, said Coyle.
I won't get nowhere.

I'd give you mine only I ain't nothing left neither.

Donny worry about it.

Need a hand?

Naw. Just to keep an eye out just in case. What I need
to do I need to do on me own.

THEY WATCHED THE ROAD till nightfall but the men
they figured on following never came. Gray dawn and
they rose quick-eyed from their beds. They washed their
faces and belted their guns and they took coffee from
the gray-haired woman who padded barefoot about
with sleepy eyes and stood awkward and sideways when
she served them. Macken went to the lean-to and fed the
horses and Faller stood from the table and walked out
onto the street. The flaxen glow of lamplight from three
windows and the moon malingered in the slate morning
sky pressing a fingernail upon it. From across the street
he watched a yellow dog shuffle towards him. The mon-
grel looked up at him and sniffed at the stranger's boots

and when Macken came around with the horse the dog nosed over to them beating the air with its tail.

They rode silent down the single street that led out of the village. The air was cool and they tightened their coats about their necks and the yellow dog began to follow and then turned its attention to the smell of something else and followed the trail curious. The village fell behind them. Large white pines that filtered the light rose to meet the riders and Faller consulted his map and they took a left turn and followed a horse trail away from the sun.

They passed a wooden cabin where a snub-nosed boy sat on a step eating an apple and he stared at the two strangers and the men did not stare back and they rode on towards a yellow hillock hunching out of the earth. They took the lean of it with the sun lighting their backs and they came to a valley and rode through it. A redstart warbled and winged overhead and settled on a tree. It fanned its tail and flashed its amber plumage and then it shook its wings away. They reached the far side of the valley where trees stood thin and it was there that Macken heard not the sound of the gun being fired or if he did he heard it only as something indistinct, an approaching murmur as the bullet that came from behind him traveled through the neck cord of his spine and came to rest in the other horse's cheek.

Macken slumped over silently in his saddle, tendrils of neck flesh ribboning his shirt as the sound of the shot smacked the air and Faller's horse collapsed upon itself throwing its rider to the ground. The sharpness of sudden pain in his ankle as Faller heard a second gunshot and he went down onto his face, crawled forward into the warm redoubt of the horse. He studied the slope of the valley until he saw the shape indistinct of a shooter on the hill. Macken's black gelding was still standing but had panicked and was dragging its dead rider about, the man dangling from the saddle and Faller saw his face which gazed blankly upside-down at the sky and he turned and took hold of a rock and lobbed it over the fallen horse. Two bullets shot a skim of dust into the air and he drew his gun and returned two shots for cover. He jumped to his feet and ran to Macken's horse, unsaddled the body which fell dully to the ground and he mounted the animal and heeled it with his spurs into a gallop and fled.

FALLER BECAME AT ONE with the beast. He rode with gritted teeth and his neck down low and his knees tucked tight till he could ride the horse no faster. Whirling dervishes of dust were hoofed up by the horse signing against the land the trajectory of his exit and he fled in the direction he had been traveling, to his left a clustered shade of bigtooth aspen and he veered hard into its grasp. The horse fluid and powerful beneath him and the ground was gnarled and dry. Currents white-hot of pain in the horse's every thundering jolt and he felt the wound wet against his boot and kicked the animal with his other leg.

The woodland cleared and beneath him he saw a dell and he rode down into the depression. Slats of sunlight through the trees and he crossed to where the ground began to rise. He continued upwards through snarling scrub, the horse panting as he nosed it at a canter and when he reached near the peak he pulled to a halt. He dismounted and tied the horse to a branch and he bent to examine the wound. The boot clinging wet to his leg and the fabric above it stewed with blood. He took the bowie knife from his belt and he sat on a rock and he took off the boot and cut at the trousers. He took a handkerchief from his pocket and he mopped the blood and then he examined the injury. The back of his calf sported a dark hole weeping, the bullet having tunneled abreast the bone to exit on the other side where the flesh hung ornate like the petals of an exotic flower.

He stood up and went to the horse and took a water bottle from Macken's saddlebag and he unscrewed the cap and slugged a long drink. Whiskey. He clenched his teeth and streamed the alcohol onto both sides of the wounded leg keeping watch on the valley below. He shucked out of his jacket and took off his waistcoat and shirt till he stood in his vest and he cut the sleeve off the shirt with the knife. He folded it and rolled it and tied it around his ankle tight and he stood up. Birds conversing in the trees and the panting lungs of the horse pneumatic and he sniffed the air deep through his nose. He surveyed the valley. A slab of shadow across the lower parts of it and then golden light where the sun warmed the trees. He saw movement and squinted his eyes and threading through the foliage he saw the blur of three men following.

He sleeved the remaining arm of the shirt and put on his waistcoat and jacket and he went to Macken's horse and pulled the breechloader from the scabbard. He checked the rifle and saw it was unloaded and he put it back in its housing. He untied the horse from the tree and guided it further up the hill to a spot twenty yards east where a rock flattened out like the infant born of some ancient butte and he tied the horse and took the breechloader and sat on the edge of the rock. He took the trigger guard and twisted it away from him and he had in his hand a ball which he put into the barrel. He poured powder behind it and closed the breech and scooped the remaining powder into the pan. He took notice of the wind and lay down on the rock and positioned his body with his elbow. He licked his finger and put it into the air and slowly closed an eye. The men were traveling below at speed and he tracked the gun sizing up the trajectory of the first rider through the trees and he waited till his breath settled and he waited for a clearing and he fired. A bird startled beneath him and flustered into the air while below the men sliced three ways but the front man he saw was still riding. Pain pulsing in Faller's leg and he chomped down on his teeth.

———————

HE RODE SWIFT THROUGHOUT the day ignoring his hunger and he kept the pace steady despite the needs of the horse he could sense was tiring beneath him. He drove the animal head-high through fields that snapped with breaking corn, across columned waves of tobacco crop that parted like the sea bright green and he made sure to leave a track he would then double back on and skirt another way. He kept as far as he could from habitation, the land hushed but for the windings of the wind and the steady thunder of the horse's hoofs. He traveled under cover of towering red cedar that stood indifferent to his enterprise and stopped on a rocky bluff and took watch upon the terrain till a half-hour passed and then an hour and he decided he had lost them and he readied to leave when he saw they were still coming.

Evening loitered then draped itself upon the sky. He met a river roaring wide and allowed the horse to drink. The water turbid and thrashing and he knew it was treacherous and he rode upstream till he met a spot less urgent where he reckoned upon a crossing. He tied his hat around his neck and everything else to the horse and the creature balked when he nosed it towards the river. The bank dived and the horse plunged neck-deep into the spangled rush, its teeth bared to the sky, and he felt the water gang upon his legs, slowly worked the horse towards the bank. It beckoned from some thirty feet and they were near halfway across when the horse faltered then fell down some invisible gully and its head was sucked underwater. He lost his grip and slipped, broke the fulvous surface of the water and went under and came back up out of it to find the horse rolling sideways, the animal pitching deeper, and he spat frigid water out of his mouth and sucked a deep breath and went down into the dim drink. Impossible to see so he felt about and put his hand on the horse's back leg that was moving and he came back up, the water white-headed rushing towards him and his head stinging and he took another breath, went under again, found the other back leg and it was moving thickly and then the horse half kicked him, a dull blow to the side of his chest and the wind went out of him and he rose to take air again, gulped it in and then back under, breasted the water around the flank of the flailing horse, put a hand on its front leg, the limb adrift and useless and he figured it was broken and he came to the surface raw from the cold, the dark shape of the horse disappearing and he turned to swim for the bank, and before he reached it he trod water to look behind him and he saw the animal come up to the surface one last time, its eyes a black piercing and lips curled over its gums mute screaming.

DOWN THE VALLEY the sun began to slide sending the dark duplicates of shadows to work alongside them, shapes that swung and hurled, contorting like ragged trees and blooming like the product of an eerie spring, an army it made of them but useless upon the land. He swung the pick and in his periphery he saw the back of Doyle and he dropped his tool and went after him, the man walking with his fists balled down the back of the scree dragging his foot behind. He called out and caught up with him and tapped the man on the shoulder and Doyle turned around with the demeanor of a man who was bothered. Coyle wiped the dust from his face with his sleeve and made a streak of dirt over his eyes and Doyle looked at him impatiently.

I'm leaving so I am, said Coyle.

So.

I need paying.

Doyle shrugged. I don't know nothing about paying nobody.

He turned around and began to walk away and Coyle stepped after him and stopped him.

Well I need paying so I do for the past few days.

Doyle eyed him cold. I ain't got no orders and I ain't got nothing to give you.

The blacksmith appeared behind Doyle and interrupted their conversation with a question of his own and Doyle turned to him and sighed and began pointing. Coyle watched them talk, looked at the dimming rim of the valley and the distance beyond and he saw the blacksmith nodding slowly with forge hammer in hand. The man turned with huge shoulders and Doyle made his leave till Coyle called out after him again.

Where's Duffy so I can speak to him?

He'll be back later.

As the evening completed the shadows of the men merged with the earth. They went below into the valley and Coyle went in search of Duffy but he was not to be found. They cooked their food over the firepits and they drank whiskey and they watched the nuns and gave them hungry looks and took weary to their tents, each man burdened now with the weight of fear as the sickness had increased all around them. Twenty men sick and seven of their number buried, no wooden caskets for the dead nor any solemn sermon as no man wanted to get involved and the blacksmith was left to do the digging. They lay in the beds, the fires outside a dying dance on the canvas of their tents, and they listened to the occasional spit of wood as the fire fell into dust.

Maurice came into the tent and lay down and after a minute he got up again and went out and when he came back to the door again he spoke.

That's it boys. I ain't hanging about.

One of the men told him to go and fuck himself then and he said he wasn't hanging about with yous fucking lot either and he asked for someone to send him out his belongings. His plate came out at arm's reach towards him and he took it and stuffed it down the back of his pants. I'm gonna take my chances and go and walk towards Philly, he said. Two shites and yous know where to stick the shovel.

The men laughed and told him he was crazy and he laughed too and said surely it was the other way round.

Coyle could not sleep and he listened to the men begin to talk and question Maurice's meaning, bother and uncertainty in their voices.

Maybe he's right, said a voice.

Naw, said another. He was outside getting sick and shitting. He should be lying down so he should.

Well I didn't come here to die, said another.

Well what are you gonna do about it?

I'm gonna follow him so I am.

Off you go then. We'll follow you.

I don't know the way.

Me neither.

I thought you wanted to go.

Aye but I want to know where I'm going first.

I'm quittin tomorrow so I am. I don't care about that Duffy so I don't.

I'll leave in the morning too.

That Duffy took us here. Why can't he take us away again?

That no good son of a bitch.

I'm going with ye but I'll not leave without my money. I didn't come here to work to be broke.

Aye we'll get our monies first.

A WARY MOON AND ITS GLOSS thin and he came upon a road and followed, a track leading darkly away from it, and he turned and followed till he came upon a farm. He tipped his hat politely to the man who answered the door warily and he told him he was lost and had an injury.

They took him in, the name's Aitken Clay, the man said offering his hand, his voice deep and familiar, and this here's my family—my wife Martha and these here are my children Mark, Matthew and little Martha minor and they're near ready for bed.

Two fair and freckled boys looked at Faller shyly and a little girl in pigtails and ribbons stared up at him and beamed.

Faller smiled thinly. I came to this area to do some hunting and in the forest somebody, I don't know who, or why, well, they shot at me, he said. Naturally I fell off my horse and the animal bolted taking all my things and this is all I have.

Martha shook her hair-bunned head and looked at him with her eyes sympathetic and blazing. What kind a fool would shoot at a man like that? she said, and her husband beside her nodded.

He looked towards Faller. Somebody not looking at what he was shooting at I'd say. We'll get you attended to mister, he said. What did you say yer name was?

John Faller.

Well Mr. Faller I'm trying to figure out. Where did this happen?

About ten miles west I do believe. I have been uncertain of my bearings all day since it happened. And now I would be obliged if you would let me fix my wound and then eat some food if you will permit me.

Martha nodded to his leg. Is that there where you were hurt?

She went out back and returned with a basin and pitcher and she put them down in front of him. She went away again and came back with some clean cloth and she bent down to help him take off his boot. He pulled his leg away from her.

I can tend to it myself thank you, he said.

He stood and took a lamp and limped out to the back step. He took off his coat and slipped the gun out of his belt and put it under the coat beside him. The steps of a child behind him and he knew he was being watched and then little Martha sat down alongside. He spoke without looking at her.

Is there a fire lighting inside, Martha minor? he asked.

Yes, said the girl.

Ask your father then to bring me a hot poker.

Why?

Be a good girl.

He moved his coat closer to his body and the girl stood up and ran inside. He sat and listened to the cicadas call the night and then he heard the wooden

boards remark when Aitken appeared on the porch behind him. Little Martha minor says you want yourself a
hot poker. Is that so's to fix your leg?

Yes. Would you mind bringing it to me? And perhaps
some alcohol if you have some.

The man paused as if to say something and he turned
on his heel and went inside and came back out with
the metal glowing. Faller turned around and seized the
iron and held it before him and with his other hand he
pinched the wound. Aitken leaned over to see, saw him
fold the skin and begin to sear it, steam serpent rising
from skin and he flinched at the sight. Faller continued
oblivious until the other side was wealed. Aitken went
inside and he came back out with a glass of whiskey
and he passed it to him and he had one for himself and
slugged it. All I got, he said.

Faller began to fold his leg in cloth and little Martha
minor walked over and sat beside him and Aitken
stepped inside. She looked up at the towering height of
him.

I'm four and one quarters. At my next birthday I'll be
five.

Faller turned and stared at her face and then he
looked at her small hands that held a jar. Inside was a
green-barked frog keeping still. She shook the jar but
the frog didn't move.

I want him to jump, she said.

Are you going to keep him in there till he dies?

The girl looked at the jar and her eyes puzzled.

I'm just keeping it.

Let me tell you something, animals don't like to be hemmed in you know.

Why's that?

It goes against their nature.

She looked at the jar and looked up at him and held it out. Would you like to take it?

No I don't want to take it.

Why not?

I don't have any use for it.

The girl frowned and she looked at the jar and stood up and ran inside. Aitken appeared behind him. I would offer you a fresh shirt but you appear to be a good size bigger than I am, he said.

I am fine as I am.

Would you like to sit at the table for some supper?

Please.

He took a piece of meat and some potatoes and a piece of corn and he began to eat them in silence. He took a loaf of bread and he sawed it and he started to chew on the crust. The children watched and whispered and the mother scolded and told them to stop whispering. The boys stopped and then they were heard again and Aitken's voice smarted. Speak up, he said. The boys went silent. Tell us what you were saying.

Nothing papa.

Martha scolded with her eyes. If it is good enough for you two to talk about it is good enough for the table.

The other boy spoke up, the words sliding awkward

out of his mouth. Mark said the man didn't say grace mama.

Faller chewed his food and then he looked up at Aitken. Fine boys you have there, he said.

Thank you Mr. Faller.

Yes. Fine boys indeed.

Tomorrow I can take you into town, Aitken said. I'll have the team hitched for an early start. I'm going in anyways as I've some things to do.

Yes that will be good.

First light, the man said. Do you mind me asking, Mr. Faller, it's just that you are not from these parts.

Go on.

What took you to these parts for hunting?

Faller sawed another slice of loaf and buttered it and he began to chew and then supped on a glass of water. He looked up at Aitken and smiled. A very troublesome creature.

Aitken looked at him and confusion lit his face and he looked at his wife and then he began to smile. Ah, the buck. Yes? Slippery creature so he is. Some fellas say the buck is more gamey. But I can detect no real difference between the meat of a doe and that of a buck myself.

Martha stood up and looked at the children.

You must excuse us, it is time to take these children to bed.

Aitken stood up and Faller stayed sitting down and as the children stood up there came three raps loudly on the front door. The family looked at each other and then they looked at Faller who was watching his food and he put his knife down and leaned back in his chair. He looked towards Aitken. Expecting? he said.

Aitken looked at his wife and she looked back. He shrugged and looked at the clock on the wall. Nope. Not at this hour.

When you go to the door and they ask you if you have anyone with you other than your own family you are to say you do not. Do you understand?

Aitken's face flashed white then crimson and his eyes went funny and Faller leaned back in the chair again and opened the side of his coat to reveal his gun.

Just in case you be thinking otherwise.

Aitken swallowed and he did not look at his wife and he turned to answer the door. They listened to the wooden boards receive his steps with a moan like the boards themselves could speak for him, then the long squeak of the door opening slowly. The voice of a man, low. They heard Aitken speak and the other man spoke a minute and then the door was closed. Faller looked at the children. Aitken returned to the room. He spoke and his voice had changed. It was tight and trembling.

I done all I can but they said they know you are here and that you ain't gone anyplace else. But they won't come in because they know I got family. Believe me Mr. Faller I don't care for who you are or for what cause these men say they want you for, for that's none of my business, but they're serious-looking men and they say they're bounty hunters so please don't do anything to hurt my children. Will you please go outside and talk with them?

Faller looked at him and leaned forward for the bread again and began to saw.

THEY WATCHED THE HANDS of the mantelpiece clock climb slowly, the pendulum licking time like a lazy lizard's tongue and nobody among that family hardly daring to breathe let alone talk and after fifteen minutes the clock took a deep mechanical breath and chimed nine. Aitken stirred and took courage and he blessed himself out loud and he began to lead a prayer and his wife and children clasped their hands and followed. Faller watched the man's chinbeard pointing upwards and the earnestness in the gray lids of his eyes that seemed to flicker imperceptibly and when they blessed themselves and were finished they opened their eyes to find Faller staring at them.

Does he ever talk to you? he said.

Aitken looked at him nervously. Who?

God.

Aitken looked at his wife and then he looked at the door. In ways, he said.

In what ways?

In the beauty that's all around us.

Faller smiled. But that's hardly talking to you directly now is it? If you died the world would go on exactly as it was before so really nobody is talking to you at all. And do you look forward to life after death?

Yes sir I do.

Well let me tell you something about that. If you were looking forward to life after death why would you be praying now?

The man's words stumbled in his mouth. Because I want my family to live. I want to live for my family.

But the fact remains is that you're afraid of dying. If your heaven was paradise and the life ever after you'd be in a rush to get there. Wouldn't you now? But you're not. Isn't that strange?

Faller looked at the children and smiled. Don't you think your parents are strange?

The children looked at him blankly.

This place called heaven, this realm of perfection and life everlasting. When it comes down to it, nobody ever wants to go there. Now isn't that strange? I'll tell you what I've seen. I've seen faith fall apart at the moment of death. I've seen people fight it in every way how. I've seen the terror in their eyes. The scratching, the squirming. If god is life ever after then why is it nobody ever wants to go to him and meet him? I'll tell you what I think. On a deep instinctive level, on a level that people prefer not to listen to, people do not believe in god. And I would have to agree.

He looked at Aitken who was sitting with his mouth open and his wife who had covered with her hands little Martha minor's ears.

Don't you think then that prayer is an amusing contradiction?

Silence swelling to take the place of the man's words and then from outside came a man's voice shouting.

You come out mister or we're comin in.

Faller stood and took off his coat and folded it and placed it on the chair. He reached down and drew his gun with his right hand and he reached into a pocket and took out extra ammunition and he put it on the table.

One more minute and we're comin.

Faller nodded in the direction of the voice. I wonder if he's religious?

Aitken blanched and he stood to move his children and Faller told him to sit and the man wavered as if the air around him had thickened right then to a mucilage miring his feet and with the effort of wading he sat down. Faller picked up his gun and tipped it forward to examine it and the family stared at it too like it was something dead or monstrous in his hand and Martha began to cry.

I told you we're coming.

THE RASP OF A DOOR opening slow on its hinges and board squeak from the men stealing in. Faller stood and turned and collared the little girl beside him with his left hand and lifted her out of the grasp of her mother clean into the air. He hoisted her in front of his body and he turned towards the door and the little girl screamed and her mother scrambled the air with her hands towards her. Faller kicked her back down and then the men from outside were coming in, their rifles pointed in the door and the first man paused as he came through to take in the sight of the girl hanging in the air in front of him and in the moment of his hesitation Faller shot him dead. The man's legs collapsed from under him and Faller dropped the child into a swing and launched her into the air at the other man taking aim with his gun and the man recoiled in horror as the child flew towards him, dropped the weapon to catch the child as she crashed into him and Faller was already on top of him as they fell to the ground and he smiled into the man's eyes and fired the other round into his head. He looked up towards the hall and took the man's rifle and swung smoothly upwards on the ball of his foot and then he was out the door.

Lamplight on the yard like spilt buttermilk. He saw the shape of another man leaping upon a saddle and he aimed the rifle and shouted at the man to hold still. The man did nothing on the horse but put his hands into the air and Faller went to him, an Indian man in a suit with long glossy hair knotted in a tail, and the man mumbled words that he was only a tracker.

Get off the horse.

The man did as he was told and he swung his leg back over the beast and when he turned around Faller shot him in the stomach. The man crumpled and fell

and curled on the ground and Faller kicked his invo-
luting body open and checked him for arms, found a
bowie knife and threw it. He went to the man's horse
and tied it to the fence and he walked around to the
back of the house where a barn stood beside it and
he went in and untied Aitken's horse. He walked the
animal around to the front and found the two horses
belonging to the dead men and he shooed those three
horses into the night and kept the Indian's horse for
himself. He stepped over the dying man and went into
the house. The family were huddled in a corner and only
Aitken wasn't crying. The two dead men lay by the door
and Faller bent to them and began to nose their pockets.
He took the men's wallets and examined their contents
and he emptied their cash and left the notes and the wallets on the table. He took his coat from the chair and put
it on and he bent down towards them, held them with a
blank stare and smiled.

HE SAT UP AND WATCHED the sun blood the canvas of
the tent. The smothered sounds of sleep and the whim-
pers of the sick. He hears also from another place the
pounding of the rain like drumming fingers and the sigh
of the soaking earth, hears the sloshing surf polishing
the bay. Thinks of the Inishowen wind curling cold on
his ears and he hears voices too, the swirl of his mother
crying when his father did not come back, the boom-
ing call of Jim, the way Sarah would gather the tinder

and bundle them into neat lines, the child hiding in the churn. Oh the small place left behind unfolding into a universe. His ear cocked to the absence of it.

HE ROSE BEFORE THE OTHERS and went to the water station and dipped the canister and slugged. Duffy usually the first about but his horse was not tied to the post. A fire began to wink at the blacksmith's small forge and he walked over to ask, met the man supping on a tin cup, his fingers black and his apron burnt. The blacksmith shook his head to the question. Haven't seen him not since yesterday.

He walked to the firepit and futhered with his hands and he looked to the west of the valley where the darkness was being stirred bright. The men staggered from their tents and they went about eating and he heard two of them say they were leaving. He watched them head off to find the foreman and then return cursing when he was not to be found.

No sign of The Cutter either and he went to look for him. He looked in the tent and went back again to the pit and the others just shrugged and then one of them said he saw him go behind the shanty and pointed. He found the man behind the tents bent on his knees and clutching. Oh god, Coyle said. The Cutter smiled weakly, his pants around his ankles and his face waxen. He whispered. Just gimme a minute.

He looked at him and bent down to help him get up

and The Cutter went to stand but was weak and fell over. Can you get me some water?

Coyle went away and came back with a canister and he gave it to The Cutter to drink. The water sluiced down the rocks of his jaw onto his shirt and when he was done Coyle took the canister back off him. The Cutter hitched up his trousers and fumbled at the button and he wiped his mouth and Coyle slung an arm underneath him. Over here. He helped him to the tent where he made him lie down and then he went off to get more water.

The morning began to stretch with no sign of Duffy and no sign of Doyle either and some of them said they were going to work regardless and they walked up to the cut. Others sat about saying they were doing nothing till they were told what to do and when they saw The Cutter was sick in their tent they told him to get out. They sat about idle, smoking their pipes and some of them watching Coyle carry The Cutter to the sick tent while others pitched into their whiskey oblivious.

The sick tent was near full, men lying on their backs with their mouths open in supplication for water, and he met the freckled face of a nun. She looked at The Cutter and pointed quietly to a place near the door for him to lie down. The Cutter holding his belly and his eyes growing glassy and distant and the only word from his lips was for water and Coyle sat down to feed him.

FALLER SAT STILL ON A ROCK on the crest of a hill, took off his boots and watched a rim of sun halo the earth. He took off his hat and scratched his head and rubbed his face and put the hat back on. A small fire crackling beside him and he inhaled the smell of smoke as he fed the flames with twigs. Above the flames on a spit he rotated a rabbit, sleeved of skin and blistering and brown and spitting fat, and he drank from a water bottle and then he took out his pipe from his pocket. He opened his tobacco tin and it was empty but for dregs in the corner and he tossed them into the palm of his hand and funneled them into the pipe. He tamped it down and took a stick from the fire and held it to the pipe and sucked on it till it flamed and he smoked what was left of the tobacco before it burned out. When the rabbit was cooked he lifted the skewered meat and put it down on the grass and he cut strips off it with his knife and he lifted the meat to his lips and blew cold air on it and chewed hungrily.

He watched the fields rufous in the reddening sun and then an awakening green. He took out his map and traced with his finger the line of the projected railway as was inked out before him and he measured the gradient of the land and folded it away. He stood and kicked dirt upon the fire with his left leg and climbed upon his horse and nosed it down through the scrub.

———————

THE MEN SAT ABOUT like they fell to where they were
sitting. A thickening of heat swarmed from the ascend-
ing sun that scattered the cold shadows at their feet.
Some of the men took to the ground and they lay there
dozing, arms rising sluggish to swat away flies from
their faces and others kept with their whiskey. Chalky
leaned idle over the fire and stoked it with sticks and
then he got up and sat away from the heat. He watched
Coyle leave the sick tent and come over to sit beside
him. Do you reckon they run off for fear?

Coyle turned his head. They didn't tell the blacksmith
if they did. He said they're coming back.

Like fuck they are.

One of the men got up, a young man called Campbell
who kept to himself beneath a ragged beard. Boys I ain't
hanging about, he said.

Some of the men turned their heads to look at him.

Is there anyone for going with me?

I'll give it one more day, a man said beside him.

Me too, said another.

I'd go with you but I want to get paid.

Aye. Wait till Duffy shows and we get our money.

Money's no good to ye when you're dead.

The others said nothing and stared at the ground.
The man said he was leaving and the rest of them could
fuck themselves but an hour later Coyle saw he was still

there. Coyle got up and went to the water station and saw it was getting low and he hitched two pails onto a pole and slung it across his back. The others watched him go to the river and no one offered to help and they watched the others up at the cut, their silence broken by the blacksmith's cart creaking by with the feet of a dead man pointing downwards over the edge.

Who was it this time? Chalky said.

Campbell looked up. Dunno.

FALLER'S LEG WAS STINGING and he sensed the horse reluctant beneath him but he nudged it on towards the ant army of men. The earth opened up before him like a scalping, men burrowing through what was left of a tawny hill and dust everywhere about. He came to a shanty and saw a trough of rust water and he took the animal to it and tied and left it there. He stood watching the camp as the horse dipped its dark nose. A spread of tents and wooden tool huts and a small smoking forge. He watched a man come out of a tent and the man stopped and took him in with a long look and then turned and walked over. The man nodded a thin smile, sleeves rolled to his elbows and dirt up to the wrists and his face tooled with deep wrinkles. Morning, he said. Can I help you?

I'm looking for a man.

Aye?

Is this here dig run by an Irishman?

The man scratched his gray temples and looked at the ground. There's some Irishmen here alright but the foreman is a fella called Jeffares and the last time I heard he was from Philly.

What do you do here?

I'm the supervisor.

I see. Do you know of any digs nearby run by Irishmen?

Well there's one or two I heard about. Do you have a name?

Faller produced the map and unfolded it. Perhaps you could show me.

I cain't be precise sure but I'll show you thereabouts.

The supervisor took the map and he narrowed his eyes and he pointed to a few places. Know for definite there's one fella there, cain't remember his name though, he said. Know who you're looking for and I might be able to help?

Faller took back the map and looked at it and then folded it and smiled. The man shrugged and turned and began to walk off and Faller called out. Do you mind if I look about? The supervisor loosed his arm into the air without turning around and called out be my guest.

He took appraisal of the dig, watched the men slam and slice the earth. He took in their faces, their complexions dark and their eyes unlooking and he saw that many of them were Chinese working free of the sun under wide-brimmed coolie hats. Nobody noticed him and if they did they paid no attention to him and he walked to where a sheet of rock lay exposed like they were unearthing the preserved remains of some remote fish upon a prehistoric seabed. He returned to his horse and mounted it and steered the animal around to the direction he had come from when he heard a voice calling out. He looked over his shoulder. It was the supervisor with his thumb in the air. Them digs are that way, the man said. Faller put his hand into the air and pointed the other way. Supplies, he said.

HE LOOKED DOWN at the big man incapacitated, his mouth agape and trying to talk and a rasp of air from his lips. Coyle leaned in straining to hear. He watched the mouth stumble over the shape of a word. A rush of air escaping. A whisper.

I canny hear you properly. You want some more water?

The Cutter wagged his finger and spoke again. The mouth puckered up, made the sound. Coyle frowned. You want me to move you?

The Cutter stared back with glassy eyes and he raised a hand and beckoned. Coyle put his ear to the twisted mouth but The Cutter said nothing and he looked about and called a nun who was attending to a man beside them. Her face plain as stone under her cornet and she sighed and came over and asked what did he want. He's tryin to say something. I canny figure.

The nun looked at him. The Cutter beckoned with his

finger and the nun leaned down and he whispered into her ear. She looked up. You have to lean into him, she said.

What's he saying?

The nun stood up and frowned and she went back to the other man. Then she spoke the words quickly. He's saying you're to leave.

HE RODE PAST A MILL HOUSE four-storey and squat by a river and forded across a covered wooden bridge. The day dimmed beneath the wooden beams and the surge of the river rode with the amplified footfall of the horse. He sensed the animal was hungry and he nudged it till the trees dispersed and the road opened upon a village. Two graybeards watched over smoking pipes. Across the street a boy with hunched shoulders hurled horseshoes towards a spike in the ground. He passed a schoolhouse and two tall white-painted houses and made for a building made of dark wood with a tavern sign sloping over the door. He dismounted and called out across the street.

Boy.

The youngster turned and met the stranger with narrowed eyes all puzzled or worried or both.

Get this horse some feed and water.

He tied the horse to the post and walked into the bar. The place reeked of men unwashed and beer long stale and two men sat at a corner table. By the fire a dog slept with a chain around its neck. A man with wire-brush gray hair leaned rotund behind the counter and he watched the stranger on his limp. Faller stood to the counter and placed his fists down upon it and nodded. Brandy and port, he said. The old man looked up at him and scratched his head. Got one, he said, but ain't got the other, but let me just go and see.

He turned and bent and searched about and came up with a bottle covered in dust. He put a tumbler on the counter and filled the glass from two bottles and Faller lifted it and walked towards the fire. He took the poker and put it in the flames and waited and ignored the men who were watching the display and he took it out and rammed it red-hot into the drink. He slugged the contents and licked his lips and put the glass back down on the counter.

Another.

The barman poured. Old war wound mister?

Faller let his gaze linger on a row of dusty bottles behind the barman's head and he watched the men behind him in the mirror now minding their own business. The barman shrugged to himself. Just askin.

Faller nodded towards the glass and smiled and the barman uncorked the bottles and filled it and he stood back from the man as if his presence now was an imposition. Faller returned to the fire and heated his drink and he went back to the counter. That'll be all, he said. He reached towards his jacket and put his hand in his pocket and held it there. He rummaged around and searched another pocket and the barman watched him with interest and Faller stopped for a moment as if he were working through his thoughts and then smiled.

I believe I have a problem. I seem to have lost my wallet in the river.

The barman raised an eyebrow. The river?

I fell in during a crossing yesterday. Lost most of my things including my horse. Had to borrow a new one.

Well you should have thought of that before you came in here drinking my liquor. The barman paused and looked into the air as if a solution that would suit the both of them were to be found hanging there.

You staying about?

Not in this area.

Well you're gonna have to pay.

Faller looked at him, noticed the man's wide nose and the pink hairless face and he stood up. How about we leave it for now? It's really only a few drinks.

The barman straightened up and scratched his chin. You can't be leaving without paying.

Faller turned to leave and the barman called out. Hey Jonah. This stranger here says he ain't gonna pay.

There was the screech of receding chairs and the sound of two men getting to their feet and the dog tapped its tail in excitement. Faller turned on his heel to meet the advancing gaze of two square six-footers, Jonah he guessed being the man older and gray who nodded to the barman. The other wore a boxer's squat nose. They looked up at the stranger. Give the man his money, Jonah said. Faller watched their hands as he spoke, saw Jonah's hands rest long and easy, the other's slowly coiling into fists.

Men this is none of your business.

It is now, said the second man.

Faller smiled. You don't want to make what's my business yours.

The men looked at each other. Jonah spoke. You might be a big feller but you ain't coming around here drinking for free the man's liquor. As he spoke the second man stepped forward swiftly swinging low his fist aimed at the stranger's stomach. Faller quickfooted a step back and in the same movement drew his gun and inverted it in his hand till he held it like a cudgel and he smashed the back of it down upon the man's face. Nose cartilage cracked and blood began to jet and the dog lunged forward barking. The man went down hollering and holding his nose and Faller turned to Jonah and spun the gun in his hand till its nostrils were pointing towards the older man's face. The man whitened and stepped back with his hands in the air staring at the weapon and the barman began to plead. I don't want no payment. No payment. Just leave that's all.

Faller turned and put the gun back in his belt and he reached over the counter for the brandy and took it with him.

Sundown and he rode towards the guesthouse with the song-pattern of cicadas entangling the air. He led the horse to the lean-to and took a few swigs from the bottle. The yellow dog followed, had watched them from the side of the road as if waiting for man and horse and it looked up at them aslant, stood wagging its tail and Faller walked past the dog's investigating nose, climbed the porch steps and went inside.

A fire burning and a stranger sat slump-shouldered beside it, spooning beans from a bowl towards a mouth hid by a few days' beard. Faller called the goitered woman and she appeared with sweat on her face and a basket of flitchings at her hip.

I want a wash in the bathhouse.

The woman nodded quickly. I'll call you when the water's heated.

Faller turned for the stairs and the woman leaned after him.

Your friend? she said.

What about him?

Will I be making supper for him too?

Not today.

Faller took the stairs with a limp and he closed the door to his room. He took a satchel belonging to Macken and nosed through the belongings. A shirt and a spoon, a spare tin of tobacco and at the bottom he found a pocket watch. He took the tin and put it in his pocket and he held the watch in his hand. It was encased in silver and on the back was an engraving, To William,

Forever, Love Kitty. The time had stopped and the glass bore a crack and he wound it between finger and thumb. He looked at it and held it to his ear and shook it but the item remained broken. He threw it back in the satchel and pitched it towards the door. The bed creaked when he sat on it and he kicked off his boots and examined his calf again. The burned flesh was black and leaking and he bandaged it up fresh and he lay down on the bed and before he closed his eyes he took a swig of the brandy.

SOFT FOOTSTEPS IN THE HALL and he sat up sharp and then a knock on the door.

Mr. Faller? Water's ready for you in the bathhouse.

He booted his feet and he took another slug and he opened the door and called to the woman who had made for the stairs. She stopped, stood shrouded in darkness, made an animal-like scuttling towards him. He gave her Macken's belongings. He saw how in the dark she still held her goitered neck with shame. Have these burned, he said. She turned then and looked at him strange.

She showed him out back to the bathhouse. It stood corrugated in the dimmed evening under a tree beside a pigpen and she hung for him a lamp inside the door. The wooden tub was wide and the edges were worn and it was filled steaming with water. She closed the door and he took his pipe out of his pocket and he put his matches by the floor. He took off his clothes and he unwrapped the cloth from his leg. He filled the pipe with tobacco and he swung a leg over the tub and eased in his large frame before following with his injured leg. Blood like dark ink flowered the water. He eased back against the tub and then leaned forward again, his pipe hanging from the side of his mouth, and he twisted his body over the side of the bath and felt about for his matches.

You looking for a light mister?

The cocking of a gun and Faller flinched and he eyed his gun on a stool on top of his clothes out of reach. From a pillar of shadow stepped the shape of a man penumbral. Not much use to you over there, the man said.

Faller swung his body back around in the bath and he stared hard at the man and smiled. That depends, he said. Have you the courtesy of a light?

The man rattled a box of matches and tossed them to him in the tub and Faller caught them mid-air. Don't get em wet, the man said. Ain't nothing more annoying than wet matches.

Faller opened the box without taking his eyes off the man and he scored a match and held the flame to his pipe. He let the match burn out slowly against finger and thumb and put it back in the box, threw them back at the stranger. He leaned back putting his hands on the side of the tub.

And you are?

Who might I be? You go upsetting folk in Philadelphia and you're sure to run into me.

Can I talk to the people who sent you?

You're talking to me.

Faller stared at the man. You working with that other party?

Only ever work for myself.

The man stepped forward and Faller recognized him as the slob he saw by the fire slurping beans. He cursed himself under his breath as he saw the man was now clean-shaven, those slumping shoulders fixed straight and his gun trained right on him.

You had time for a shave, he said.

No point in being unprofessional.

I suppose now you want me to put on my clothes and travel back with you to Philadelphia?

That ain't gonna be necessary, the man said.

Faller kept staring, sucked deep on his pipe, the smoke burling downwards to plume heat in his lungs, and he held it inside him in contemplation. He blew it back out, a steady stream thickening in the direction of the other man. Each devours the other, he said. That's the way it is don't you think?

I guess so.

He leaned down and put the smoking pipe on the slatted ground and he took a rag and a bar of yellow soap and he oiled the rag and took to washing. He ran the cloth lengthways down the reaches of his arms and he washed underneath his armpits and he scrubbed the slab of his great chest and then he oiled his face and rinsed it. When he was done he tucked his knees towards him and cleaned his legs and he reached forward and washed his feet. He folded the rag and put it on the ground and he leaned back in the bath.

I've come to notice that whatever calculations we make in life are destroyed by accidents or agencies beyond our control. Don't you think that's true?

The man didn't answer.

You really do have to think about that. All this nonsense about destiny being our own. How parochial. Every man, every nation, thinks they have control over a world that throws them about like a high wind. I'll tell you, there's always an agency more powerful than your own. Think about that. The terrible beauty of it. How it lies there unseen waiting for you. Every fate, every life, every story swallowed by forces greater. Mine now a part of yours. Yours a part of someone or something else's when the time comes. So on, ad infinitum. That's all there is to it.

Faller began to lean forward, hunched his shoulders.

The man let the words hang in the air and silence walled between them and then the man spoke. Yer a pretty strange fella to be in the kind of business that yer in. But you know I spend a lot of time on my own thinking betwixt me and the saddle and I ain't come up with much but I did come up with this—the difference between man and beast is we're able to imagine the future and they're not. But what makes us no better than em is we cain't predict it. That's there where the problem lies. And just in case yer wondering, you can run for your gun, but this flintlock here fires in triplicate.

Faller looked up at the man, fixed his eyes on him and smiled. Yes indeed.

He put his hands on the side of the tub and stood slowly his immense frame upon it, slabs of water sluicing off the white flanks of his flesh and he stood there smiling and naked, the orbs of his eyes huge upon the man, began to climb slowly out of the tub, the gunman taking a step back, I warned you now, not another step further, Faller continuing with his eyes fixed upon the man, stepping out of the bath like something colossal that moved outside the confines of measured time, a primeval heaving, wetly, slowly, and then he was upon his gun.

SHE HEARD THE SHOTS—one-two—and she waited and heard three and she put down her broom and traveled light-footed to the door, peered through a small crack into the gloom. She saw the man out back and watched his movement, the way he dragged backbent the body of a man that looked too heavy, his hands yanked into armpits that socketed loosened limbs, a mass being heaved against the idle intentions of dead weight. The friction of dragging feet and the man came to a stop at the chicken wire fence. The man dropped the body to the ground and he went to a fence post and kicked it loose and he lifted it out of the ground. He disinterred two more posts until the earth was hollowed like a mouth untoothed and she saw the man bend down again and seize the body under the arms. He dragged it further and then he stopped and he began to roll the corpse, resplendent in its selenic and soaking nakedness, towards the torpid pigs.

MIDNIGHT WAS LONG PAST when the horseman ghosted into the camp. The animal noiseless as if it knew the needs of its rider who dismounted in the dark by a spidery tree. He slipped like shadow about the place till he found them in two pairs sleeping, saw the indigo whites of their habits, and he nursed them awake and told them with a growl to shush. Your work here is done, he said, and he made them get up and made his intentions clear with the rib-prodding barreled steel of his gun.

THE MEN AWOKE in the gloom of dawn, each man glad he was still physical. They sat blurred at the firepit and they were low on supplies and the whiskey was near all gone and they looked at what was left and some of them pitched into it. The rest scratched about or huddled in groups and looked expectant towards the mouth of the valley for sign of Duffy though each one knew in the reaches of his being the contractor would not come back. No one wanted to say it but they as good as did when it was discovered the nuns had quit too. They took the news like men inured to surprise and sat back down with what they were doing, which was not much at all.

They stood idle or sat about gambling but their hearts were not in it, for each man secretly was wondering if he too would get sick and then one of them stood and nodded towards the mouth of the valley. There's a man coming on a horse, he said. They turned and watched the rider approach, a cloud of dust hoofed behind the animal. The horseman wore a neckerchief over his face and his hat over his eyes and they saw the horse was dragging something. The rider neared the swale where the shanty sat and he pulled up short at the perimeter. They watched him unhitch a rope and throw it to the ground and he turned and rode away. The men stood up and walked over to where he had stopped and they saw he had left a body. It lay face down in the dirt noosed about the neck and Chalky turned it over with his toe. The man's complexion was scratched raw and teeth were broken and gums were bleeding and they saw it was the body of Maurice. Beneath the blood his lips were gray and his eyelids brown and his extremities dark with his own fecal matter. The men stood stunned and the blacksmith wandered slowly over and he looked at the body. He sighed, rubbing his moustache with the back of his hand, and walked away and he returned nursing an old mule and cart. He loaded the body upon it and Coyle watched him and walked over. What in the hell? he said.

Again the blacksmith sighed. There's people about who'd like you lot to keep to your own, he said. That's just the way it is. And he turned and led the mule away.

Coyle went to the sick tent and tended to The Cutter, noticed how the man had weakened. His body strung out and his eyes far-flung like the eyes of a man watching from someplace remote, his breath a mere supplement to his being. He looked at the other sick men shrunken and dry like wizened wood sea-shored and then The Cutter turned to him and whispered. Coyle leaned in to hear.

Talk to me, The Cutter said.

Tell ye what?

Anything.

Coyle looked at him puzzled and then he spoke.

I remember something of a dream from the night. Been thinking about it all day. It was so real it was like I was there you know? Like I took a piece of it with me.

The Cutter looked at him. Where were you? he said.

Coyle smiled. It was a morning bursting bright so it was and I was in the forest, the axe in my hand and the wood all coined thickly about me. And in the dream I knew I had come home.

The Cutter whispered again, his voice near inaudible. My pocket.

Coyle leaned over him and reached a hand into the man's pocket and took a hold of something his fingers

recognized immediately for what it was by touch alone
and he took it out. The ribbon.

The Cutter whispered. On the road. Never got time.

Coyle just staring at it and then his fist closed around it.

Go on, The Cutter said. Go home.

Coyle opened his fist and folded the ribbon and put it
in his pocket and he took a hold of The Cutter's hand
and he squeezed it tightly. Ye bollox ye.

HE STRODE THROUGH the dig, past the men sitting
slumped and he gave them nothing of a farewell, told
them nothing of his intentions, that he was going to escape the figure of death on his trail, that he was going to
get home, that he had a wife and daughter to behold and
he would do so, but as he walked up the red-rubbled hill
his thoughts began to weigh upon him and as he neared
the top he had to sit on a jut of rock to think.

He thought of his wife broken on the bed and the
early morning light of the cottage and the smallness of
his child. No bigger almost than his hand, mucus filmed
about her body and the eyes of her not yet opened. A
beauty. The midwife spoke that he wasn't to be allowed
in but he took no heed and watched her take a knife to
the cord on the child's belly, cut it to give the child life
independent, joy like light bursting to escape his body.
He thought too of his father and when he was a child
and the calm encouragement from the man to burrow
an arm inside the animal, the grasp of shank and then

a yank till life tunneled outwards towards him, life vis-cid and blue-gasping and his father breathing life into it with his own mouth and he stood there watching, his pride swelling.

He saw below him the valley torn raw while men sat like stones in loose circles and the thought then came upon him. I canny leave a dying man. Canny do it. And he looked at the sky as if he could learn something from it but what he saw had nothing to say and he took the ribbon out of his pocket and he looked at it, and he saw the face of his wee girl and he made a promise to him-self, brought the ribbon to his lips, and he put it then in his pocket, stood up and began to walk back down.

YOUS BOYS, HE SAID. There's help needed here for these men. They can't be left on their own. We got to get them out.

He watched his voice wash over them, the men wear-ing a look that spoke silent of their indifference and he turned and he picked up two pails. He went to the culvert spanning the stream beneath the fill and doused both till brimming. Each sick man who could drink he gave a sup of water to and with a cloth he dampened their heads. When he was done he walked to a barrow and he tipped the earth out of it and wheeled it back to the tent.

The sky so cloudless it seemed the lids of the earth were peeled for the sun to hammer the air. The men watched him struggle, the weight of The Cutter unbalancing him on his heels, and he dragged the invalid by the underarms. He got him to the barrow and he pitched him into it and began wheeling and wobbling towards them. He came abreast of them and stopped.

Don't yous realize we're done for if we stay here?

The men responded with blank dark faces, their mouths dumb and their eyes fixed awkward to someplace else.

There's four more sick yesterday and that brings the number to near half the group, forgetting the eight now that passed. Load these boys up and we'll go back to Duffy's house and help get these boys fixed and get paid for ourselves because we're not going to get our worth sitting here. You're no good to nobody like this.

The men looked at Coyle and at The Cutter draped near-dead in the barrow.

One man stood and spoke. It was Thompson. The man's right. But we should leave them ones here and go ourselves. We'll only get a dose of it.

You can leave but yous will be no better than the others that did, Coyle said.

I ain't said I was any better than anyone.

Chalky stood up stiff and leaned his gray old eyes on Thompson's tight-lipped face and then turned and pointed down the site.

We can carry them in those.

He began walking with his arms sticking out like some kind of scarecrow and Coyle turned and went after him. Some of the men stood and others reluctantly followed. The men who stayed as they were watched sullen, some of them with their arms folded while others pretended not to be looking. They untied a dozing mule and marshaled a worn-out dappled horse and hitched them to a pair of carts and they ignored the wondering stare of the blacksmith. Coyle about-turned the mule and led it to the sick tent.

The men went inside and began to carry out the sick men. Their faces contorting out of fear and disgust but they lifted them up onto the trucks anyway and they shut their ears to the sound of the groaning. They were carrying one man when somebody said to put him down and they did so and leaned over him.

The man who spoke bent down and he rested the back of his hand upon the fellow's mouth, lips like dry paper.

This one here's dead boys.

They stood and looked at the body. His lips a bluey brown and they were drawn back over his gums leaving him in death with a crooked smile.

Somebody go an close his eyes.

The man on his haunches leaned forward and smothered them shut.

We canny go nowhere till we bury him.

For sure.

Some of the men left the sick men in the carts and they carried the dead man dangling four-square till they reached the fill. It leaned up from them some ten feet and the earth was scarred where the blacksmith had dug graves. He loped over to them sad-faced with a shovel in his hand and began to pitch in. When the hole was dug he leaned back on his tool and began to rub his horseshoe moustache.

No more wood. Just put him straight in.

The body laughed at them with its rictus grin and they spaded the earth on top of it, the clay clumping about the corpse and crumbs falling into the dead man's mouth. Dust rose hotly from the pit and it glittered as it stirred skywards and the men covered their eyes against it. When they were done the blacksmith sleeved sweat from his brow and he nodded down to the shanty.

How many of ye are standing? he said.

Less than half, said Coyle.

Yez are gathering about to leave then?

Most of us.

You be careful now with that. And then he looked over his shoulder. I got the dinner waitin on me.

Up towards the neck of the ravine they traveled like a procession of ragged penitents stumbling under the weight of their sins. Dust danced and spilled off the shaking carts that became to them an ensemble of limbs while a man blood-wild with whiskey danced knees high and demented. The land leaned up towards the sun while the heat came down upon them and smothered the air on their breath.

The carts complained to the dull music of the animals' hitching and the men kept their silence till one looked upwards the valley where out of the gleam of sun he saw someone move. There's men awaiting up there, he said. Before them loomed the shapes of others, men on strong horses with guns lap leaning and the minds of the workers puzzled over what kind of trouble this was. They continued up the slope till they came near the top and a horse was stepped forward, the rider gray-haired with pitted cheeks, and he put his hand flat into the air and hollered at them.

You boys ain't going nowheres.

Hesitance in their heels but the procession nudged on till the man called out to them again. You hear me you sons of bitches? You ain't moving another step.

The men at the front brought the animals to a halt and they studied the assembly before them. The countenance of clean men with neckties about their faces and Coyle saw that one of them was the farmer from before.

Not another step I tell you, the leader said. Take yer sickness back down with you where you belong and not a damn sight near the good folk from round here families and all. You lot are staying put in the valley and if you think you aren't hell will come paying. You hear me? I tell you. A pack of diseased dogs.

Two riders beside him edged forward. One of them hawked phlegm and lowered his neck scarf and spat down towards them. The animals strained on the hill to contain the weight of their load and some of the men figured the man for bluffing. They looked at each other for answers till one man started forward, the others unsure but for the man leading the mule who watched and began to follow. The two horsemen brought their guns into the air and one of them fired a shot over the workers' heads and the animals startled at the sound. The men ducked low but for the walker who eyed the men straight and he kept walking till a horseman in plaid on top of a chestnut gelding raised his gun from his lap and fired. He had taken aim at the man's head and the shot took the man's ear clean off. A single drop of blood blotched the man's shirt and he stared at it incredulous. He put his hand to his ear and pulled it back sodden and puce and he fell to the ground with shock and in the space after the shot as it ringed the air the pack animals took to revolting. Coyle pulled tight the reins of the horse, whispered to it, nursed it steady, but the mule nearby startled so badly it turned as if to leave, the cartload locked deadly to its body, and it tipped itself over and the cart with its cargo of men. The man who was shot climbed crimson from the ground, a ragged slab for where his ear once was, and he crabbed down the valley, others around him scuttling backbent while those that were left surrendered their hands to the air.

The gunmen above said nothing, just watched as they allowed the men to recover the sprawl of bodies from under the wreckage of the neckbroken mule, each man lifted up and put on the remaining cart though some of them saw they were dead.

THEY TOOK BODIES of those that were living and those that were dead and they laid them on the ground, who was alive now it was difficult to tell. Afterwards they did not know what to do but sit so they sat together and watched the sky, the great blue permanence winged high with white, and they looked upon the silent banks of the valley wondering upon the nature of their horror. They wanted nothing to do with the others who had chosen to stay and who sat mute nearby, stunned at the earlier spectacle and too ashamed to talk. When they grew hungry some of the men stood and went to the fire, the outcasts sitting about, and no sooner were they there than they began throwing their fists.

The man with the ribboned ear sat on his own supping whiskey with sackcloth folded to his head and they watched him get up and worry about and sit back down again and they were not sure if he was laughing or crying for the air was taut with madness.

Coyle went looking for The Cutter and he found him laid out between two others and he saw that he was dead. He bent down to him and felt the skin of his cheek cooling despite the heat of the ground and he closed the man's eyelids.

He heaved the body up till it was bent over his shoulder and he carried it through the valley. He placed it down by a poplar tree and he walked towards the work sheds. He found a sledgehammer and swung it at a building till the wood blistered then burst and when it was taken apart he took a hammer and punched the wood clean of its nails. He cut and hammered the timber into the shape of a box and when it was built he stood it and hugged his arms around it. He walked it towards the valley fill and placed it down on the rubbled land and he went back and lifted the body and heaved it over his shoulder.

Over the west wall of the valley the day was fading and he took a shovel and began to dig. The land heedless, dense with loam and stone, teeth of rock snarling out of the dust, and he dug a hollow three foot deep. He put the body of The Cutter in the box and worked it down into the hole and then he stood above it. The earth corrupt before him and filled with violence.

IT WAS STRAIGHT AFTER *talkin to Wee Paddy Doherty that I went looking for Bridie, went to her family home in Ballyliffen, and they told me she'd gone. She'd left to get work in Tyrone they said and I asked about and got a lift to Strabane from a kindly man who was going all the way to Monaghan from Derry. I had her address and found where she was workin—a big farmer's house about ten miles out past the town.*

A white two-storey building so it was and it had a dog guarding it that nearly chewed the leg off me but I kept on walkin. Nearly chewed the leg off me so it did. I wasna sure what she looked like but when I saw her I remembered her face from about. A wee quiet woman so she was with shining blue eyes and a tiny chin like she was hunching into herself and she'd tell you everything in a whisper. When I told her where I'd come from she said she didn't want to talk about it at all and she gave a sad smile and closed the door in my face.

I felt wild let down so I did and left, the dog barkin at me but keeping his distance, and I was down the road out past the gates when I heard her call out and next thing there she was behind me. She was runnin towards me bunchin her skirt and she said she was sorry but she didn't want any trouble out of it and she said she knew who I was and why I needed to know.

She told me she always had ears to what was going on and she knew almost everything that happened in the

*house and I asked her why the trouble happened and she
looked at me and then she just shook her head.*

*She said that Hamilton was nothing but bother
drinkin all the time and gamblin away his father's
money and he wasna right in the head either. Then she
said that there was no good reason for it, no good
reason at all. And I remember I began to cry again I
couldna help it and I said to her what did she mean. And
she looked at me and her eyes began to get wet too and
she took a hold of my wrist and I remember her hand
had a chill in it that I could feel right to the bone and
she said she was in the scullery one time and she over-
heard Hamilton talkin to Faller, telling him he wanted
Coll out. And Faller was ignoring him because that was
the kind of him and Hamilton was always trying to im-
press him and then Faller asked him finally what he had
done and Hamilton said he had passed Coll on the road
that same day and Coll did not doff his hat.*

MAYBE THERE IS some plan for us we canny figure on but I'm worn out lookin. Coll's mother told me before she died—ach the memory of her all weak like that now I donny want to be thinking about it. But before she passed she told me that all you can do in this life is to learn to accept loss. I always thought about that afterwards thinking she were wrong but I'm worn out now from hoping to see him again and I figure maybe she were right. You come into this world with nothin and you canny leave with anything. But I got to be strong for the children so I do and I got to keep hoping that he's going to come back and that's all there is to it. I mean would you just look at him Brigid, look at the wee rosy red cheeks on him, just the spit of him. And I named him after his father. Isn't he a sight?

THEY SAT SEALED in the darkness, huddled as before in their separate groups and the air hot as hell. Their faces lit by trembling fires and the hollows of their eyes were pooled in shadow as if in their eyes it was the darkness of death that lay. Discord in their relations and turmoil in their hearts and they listened to the land silent and the crackle and spit of the fire and they heard the calls of those that had since begun to sicken. Men went crawling in the gloom for a place to void while the others around them heard their moans and tried not to listen. They drained the last jugs of whiskey into their cups and then drank the water and nobody was hungry.

Atop the valley he watched torch fires glimmer and move about slowly like fat fireflies. The sky vivid with stars and he could see the shapes of sickening men coiled about the place and to the east a bank of dark cloud slowly lidding.

He went to the tent and he lay down with the others to sleep. Closes his eyes. Lies in the lulling of memory and falls into the black hole of it and she turns and smiles and he is with her now and there is nothing to the night. He walks ageless up the stony path underneath the bending blackthorn blossom. Light now, an afternoon. The light golden and he smoothes her hair. Light on the nape of her neck and he holds her hand and warm is her flesh. Dog rose and elder and the bees dip drunk on the air scented sweet. The tinkling mirth of a small stream and they step over it, step past a house pale and unwatching, walk up the hill till halfway they sit. Glashedy island risen rocky out of the water, old man's head of the sea watching whitely the winging birds. The earth, the air and the sea and she whispers into his ear breathily.

And he thinks. That this was it.

And he noticed he was awake and he sensed others were too. The air stagnant with heat and he saw some of the men sitting up and listening. He trained his ears to the low rumble coming from behind them and then someone stood up and shouted. Horses. And then it was upon them and it awoke to him what it was. The first report rolled off the valley in clattering shocks and another followed as the men surged out of the tent. All around them the stomping of hoofs and the blurring of torch fires wielded by horsemen encircling them, the maneuvers of some crazy war dance. He saw a man come down off a horse with a rifle in his hand and he sighted it walking into a tent that pulsed a moment later with a shock of white light, a momentary illusion as if it had been flared by sheet lightning before it was sucked into the darkness again. He heard the clatter of gunshot that followed and the tent illumined again and went dark and the air around him began to pulse with bitter light, thunder from firing guns and men began to scream. Everywhere he saw men with death grins wielding rifles from the neck and some of them by the side while others held torches so the shooters could see, the ground glowing red like coals beneath them. He ducked low and ran across the swale, guns snorting acrid fumes that curled invisible towards the sky and he heard them calling to each other, working the shanty in a circle, and he heard his own kind, men calling for mercy unheeded and then he snagged and stumbled over a body. He picked himself up and pitched atop another and the figure moaned under his weight. The wetness of the man's blood warm against his hands and he crawled desperate and her face appears before him, more vivid than he has imagined and he is struck by the intensity of it, and he continues to crawl but he does not know where he is, everywhere it seems lie more bodies and the ground is biting at his hands and gnawing at his knees and he hears her voice softly, and he crawls harder, the night air a clamor of pounding anvil around him and he comes smack up against the standing legs of another. He turns and scrambles backwards and then he puts his arms over his head as if to shield him from what the man standing over him intends to do, sees the gun rising and he hears her voice over the sound of the shot and it is clear to him now what has become of him, a wallop like the kick of a horse to his side and his hands fall back useless. A fierce ringing in his ears and still he hears her voice softly, lie here my love, lie here against the warmth of my skin, and he lies into her then, the warmth wet at his side, lies back to sleep against the turning of the earth.

ALONE THE BLACKSMITH WORKS, slowly and with care. Just a shovel and his two bare hands and he digs the earth deep till it lies open and receiving. The morning spent and the rubble around him red and he looks at the pit and thinks it has to do. He passes the day struggling under their weight, each one trouble enough for one man, and when he has enough for a cartload he nurses the horse forward up towards the valley fill, the animal slow upon its dusted hoofs. It stands patient with low-bowed head while the man unloads the cart, each one first he puts onto his back and then he lays them gently upon the ground. When he is finished he turns the horse around and begins the trip again. All day he works as the sun crests the sky and then begins to fall and though he is hungry he does not stop to eat and he stops only to give the horse some water. The horse struggles to cart forward the last load and then the blacksmith makes it stop and he empties the cart and he stands there alone before slowly with his shovel he begins to close over the earth.

He bends to the firepit and lights a wooden torch and puts it to the shanty. The canvas smokes and catches fast as he lights each tent and then the whole place is burning, chutes of black smoke sent bitter into the air, and he turns through the blackened pools that mirror the blaze and begins walking. And then he sees. Lying gray in the mud—a ribbon. And he bends to pick it up, wipes the smear of wet dirt off it, holds it for a moment in wondering and then he lets it go, taken off his hand by the breeze.

The day then is done under a soundless sky and he looks up and sees red sky of evening. The west festooned with coming night and rain clouds thick and waiting. The breeze sighs long, shakes the leaves that lie strong on the bough awaiting the return of autumn. The land steps into shadow and the birds tuck their heads. All then is still till the clouds burst open, rain that begins to fall great and unheeded. The land is old and tremulous and turns slowly away from the falling sun.

Epilogue

IT WAS A MORNING BURSTING BRIGHT SO IT WAS AND he was in the forest, the axe in his hand and the wood all coined thickly about him. He sent the axe into the sky and sank it quarter into the stump and in the dream he began to walk for home. Dew on the fields and he glossed his boots, the day just hung, a white saturate that told nothing of what was to come, no rain nor wind just a great stillness about and the silence broken by the faint reach of a dog's barking. And he followed the path, bright upon the lane, bright upon the beech tree, came to a bend and stood listening, the morning near hushed, scent of earth and sap, and onwards he went, upwards the hill, a pebble glanced and sent rolling, and when he got to the door he shook off his boots and placed his feet on the slate step, his hand on the latch, and he heard the sound of their voices warmly and went in.

Acknowledgments

Gerard Stembridge and Hugo Hamilton for being generous and wise early readers. Shaun McLaughlin and Sean Toland for subjecting the book to local scrutiny.

Peter Lahiff, Richard Oakley, Ian Devlin, Donal O'Sullivan, Gavin Corbett, Declan Burke, Birch Hamilton and Jim Kelly for their help and support.

All the staff of the late *Sunday Tribune* for giving me a starting point. Mary Rose Doorly for pointing me in the right way. Sinéad Gleeson and Charlotte Greig for lighting the path. Ivan Mulcahy for taking the leap, and for being the kind of agent authors dream about— dynamo and sage.

My editor at Quercus, Jon Riley, his assistant Richard Arcus, and at Little, Brown, William Boggess and Asya Muchnick, for their passion and insight.

My mother and father Mary and Pat, my brother Derek and sister Louise, for their love and encouragement.

Anna for her unstinting love and support.

Thank you.

About the Author

Paul Lynch is an Irish novelist and critic. He has written for Ireland's *Sunday Tribune*, the London *Sunday Times*, the *Irish Times*, the *Sunday Business Post*, the *Irish Daily Mail*, and *Film Ireland*. He lives in Dublin.

LYNCH   CEN
Lynch, Paul,
Red sky in morning :a novel /

CENTRAL LIBRARY
01/14